A

PHILOSOPHY

OF RUIN

A NOVEL

NICHOLAS MANCUSI

HANOVER
SQUARE
PRESS

**HANOVER
SQUARE
PRESS**

Recycling programs
for this product may
not exist in your area.

ISBN-13: 978-1-335-93066-8

A Philosophy of Ruin

Library of Congress Cataloging-in-Publication Data has been applied for.

HanoverSqPress.com
BookClubbish.com

Printed in U.S.A.

For JMO

A

PHILOSOPHY

OF RUIN

"Misfortune in general is the rule."

—Arthur Schopenhauer, *On the Suffering of the World*

PART I

1

2009

Oscar Boatwright's mother had died in her seat during a flight from Hawaii to California, and his father had been made to sit for three hours in the same aircraft as her cooling body. This information had been relayed to Oscar via telephone by an airline representative who spoke in a managed tone that simultaneously conveyed measured sympathy and complete legal indemnity. The plane was still in the air.

It was an hour drive to the airport, and Oscar decided that the best course of action was to compress his emotions into a small square feeling in the middle of his solar plexus, to be dealt with as soon as possible, but not until after he had picked up his father. As he sat in silence by himself during the drive, he felt his emotions begin to armor themselves, or perhaps flee the field entirely.

★ ★ ★

Now Oscar stood at the gate with another airline employee who wore a white short-sleeve shirt with epaulets and golden trim. The man had met Oscar at the terminal and explained several things while Oscar took off his shoes and belt and they walked through security. What he had said was doubtlessly important, but Oscar hadn't listened, or had already forgotten. They stood silently as ashen-faced travelers passed them on their way to meet their drivers, each imbued with an awful power by the story they would soon tell of what they had seen on the plane.

Through the terminal's cathedral-tall panes of glass, Oscar could see an ambulance out on the tarmac. Its sirens and lights were not on. Above him, the airport PA announced an imminent departure.

At the top of the ramp appeared his father, Lee Boatwright, flanked by two more airline representatives, slightly softer at the edges than the last time Oscar had seen him fourteen months ago. He wore a blue Hawaiian shirt. One of the men at his side had his carry-on.

"Dad, Jesus Christ," Oscar said.

One of the reps was saying something to the effect that he would like to take them to see someone in an office.

"Oh, Oscar. It was just like that." Lee snapped his fingers. "There was a terrible scene."

For the rest of the day, Oscar and his father were conveyed through the halls of a nightmarish, half-corporate, half-governmental bureaucracy that in its cold and comprehensive knowledge of all things, such as how deep vein thrombosis attacks the human body or how lawsuits tended to be fruitless in these scenarios, seemed to contain the truth of the world in total: violent, indifferent and almost entirely explicable. While Oscar listened to a doctor and several lawyers explain how they believed his mother had died and their innocence in the matter, he could only marvel at the fact that people could be doing their jobs so effectively, at a time like this, when people's mothers were dying. *What a tremendous gap separates our consciousness*, he thought.

Finally the two men were delivered onto the curb in the Pacific twilight, along with two large pieces of luggage: blue and red, his and hers.

In the car, Oscar asked his father why he hadn't told him that they were planning on visiting. In fact, Oscar wasn't even aware of their vacation. As far as he had known, his parents had still been more or less happily ensconced in their split-level ranch in Indiana, the same house in which Oscar had been raised, where his father watched lots of cable news, his mother led a book club with other teachers from the middle school, and they both attended Knights of Columbus functions and played Hearts with the Andersons on Thursday nights.

"We wanted it to be a surprise," Lee said, looking at his hands.

"You know that that would've upset me."

"Oh, I'm not so sure."

"I'm telling you that it would."

"Whose car is this?"

"My friend's."

A moment passed and Oscar realized that his father was crying, although he hadn't made any sound. Oscar tried not to look over, as he didn't know what his father looked like when he cried, and didn't care to learn.

"They put a blanket over her," Lee said, "but it didn't cover her feet. Her little white shoes. It's all I can think about."

It was dark when they got back to Oscar's faculty apartment. Oscar was an assistant professor of philosophy, with a focus on metaphysics when he wasn't teaching intro, which, this early in his career, represented the majority of his course load. He put water on to boil for coffee and got a microwavable pizza out of the freezer. His father sat down at the kitchen table, which was really the only table in the little place.

This was how American families dealt with death: a pot of coffee, a phone in the middle of a kitchen table, a box of tissues, a yellowed photo album. Once, prior to a certain year, mourning would have also involved cigarettes. But their scene contained no family; just a man and his father, a line rather than a tree, and so far from their real home, where the photo albums that Oscar wished were now on hand could be found wedged into a bookshelf. Nobody would be coming to the door with casserole here. The local paper that would run an obituary mentioning her years as an English teacher and her community service in the Catholic church would not be seen by any eyes within two thousand miles.

"This is…so strange," Lee said. "I feel like I'm dreaming."

"We're both still in shock," said Oscar.

"I suppose so."

"She was such—God, the past tense."

Lee winced. "Let's not make this harder than it is."

Oscar felt a twinge of some old emotion that he associated

with being ten years old. He couldn't name it precisely—
something anger-adjacent.

"Dad," Oscar said, much more for his father's benefit than
his own, "would you perhaps like to pray with me?"

"No, I think not right now, thank you."

"Okay. Why don't you change out of that Hawaiian shirt."

Lee made phone calls, first to his friends from the Knights
of Columbus, and also to the Andersons, his neighbors of
twenty-five years. (Some of these people might not have expected that they were on the shortlist for death calls, but the
Boatwrights had few relatives, and none that they kept up
with.) Oscar watched as his father progressively edited his
grim news down to its most economical form. It only took
one pass for Lee to realize that he wasn't required to mention
that it had happened on a plane, and by his third call he was
getting through the pertinent facts in around three minutes,
with promises to call again soon, while still staying on the
line long enough to receive condolences.

Oscar sat there not drinking a mug of coffee. When his
discomfort with the call that had not yet happened, the one
that should have been made first, became too large to bear,
he held out his hand for the receiver.

"Here, I'll do it if you can't."

Lee kneaded his face in his palms and spoke through his
fingers.

"Okay."

Oscar thought for a moment, took a sip of coffee and dialed.

Oscar's older sister still lived in Indiana, where she was married to a successful businessman and mother to three young

kids. Her husband was by all appearances and accounts a good man and good to her, but he read exclusively nonfiction about things like how to dominate a meeting with body language, and so Oscar assumed that he and his brother-in-law looked down on each other from different doctrines of living with a mixture of jealousy and distrust. When she answered the phone instead of him, Oscar was relieved.

"Gracie, it's Oscar," he said, and then he told her. She screamed and dropped the receiver, and after a second picked it up again.

"What? What do you mean?" she said.

"We're told that it was probably painless," Oscar lied.

"On a plane? Where is she now?"

"Did you know they were in Hawaii?" Oscar said, and shot a look at his father.

"Hawaii? This is crazy. I don't understand you."

"Dad's coming back home in two days. Can you be at the house?"

"When are you coming home?"

"As soon as I can. I have to figure a few things out."

"Yeah, I can be there. No, they didn't tell me they were going anywhere. Oh, God."

"I know."

"This is terrible."

"I know."

"I'm going to cry so much. Jesus. How's Dad?"

"He's sleeping." He tried to look his father in the eyes, to twist the knife, but Lee's eyes were down in his coffee. "He told me to tell you he loves you."

★ ★ ★

Oscar gave his father his own bed for the night. They said good-night and hugged briefly, which, he realized, was the first time they had touched that day.

There were stacks of books and ungraded student papers covering the couch, which reminded him, after this twelve-hour nightmare, of the existence of his life. He moved everything to the coffee table so that he could lie down, pulled his laptop onto his chest, and booted it up, bathing his face in fuzzy white light. The thirty unread emails in his inbox seemed entirely unconquerable, and dread installed itself inside of him alongside the shock and burgeoning grief. After he sent a message to his classes to inform them that they wouldn't be meeting tomorrow, he closed the laptop and was about to let it slide off onto the floor when he remembered that he couldn't afford to replace it if it broke, and rested it on top of an aesthetics anthology.

Lee came back out of the bedroom and stood in the doorway, holding on to the jamb. He was in his underwear, boxers and a T-shirt, and black socks.

"Son, I feel like there are things that we should have said to each other today, but I don't know what they are. We'll try again tomorrow."

Oscar hated everything about this. "That's all right, Dad. I understand. Good night."

"Well. Good night." Lee rapped his knuckle on the doorframe as he turned around and shut the door.

Oscar lay back down and stared up at the ceiling in the darkness. He pulled a blanket over his body, just to feel its weight, and went through several different mental exercises he had developed for whenever he felt particularly confident that everything was terrible and the universe was hell.

He tried to distance himself from the idea of reality existing outside of his own head.

He tried to meditate on the best arguments against the existence of free will, hoping to surrender his power over the situation and the way that he felt about it into the firm embrace of hard determinism.

He tried to find relief in the fact that eventually he would be dead and that, in all likelihood, all of this would be proven not to have mattered, even a little.

Finally, in desperation, he prayed to the bearded God of his boyhood, addressing him directly, reciting the prayers that he had repeated so endlessly in his youth, Hail Marys and Our Fathers.

And then he thought, to hell with it, and at last permitted himself to look plainly on the long unfairness of his mother's life.

When Oscar turned on the television so that his father wouldn't hear him sob, there was only static.

2

He woke up bleary and unrested to the sound of his father fumbling with the coffee maker. He hadn't slept deeply enough to dream, but he had at least lost a few hours. "Here," Oscar said, and got up to take the pot away.

It was still early. They sat at the table and ate freezer waffles in silence. Oscar thought that the only way he was going to get through this day was to focus on logistics first, physical things that needed doing, and save the emotional accounting for later.

His father, accustomed to dressing early out of habit, sat across from him in khaki shorts, scuffed loafers, and a white oxford. Oscar was still wearing the same clothes as yesterday. His mother's luggage sat unopened by the door.

"How did you sleep?" Oscar asked after several minutes, and his father did his little quarter-laugh, a kind of sharp exhalation through the nose.

"I don't suppose that's a real question."

"Come on, Dad, I don't know."

Oscar realized that eventually they'd have to broach the topic of the transport of the remains.

The unreality of this astounded him. He could feel, and almost even see, his grief as something apart from him, as if it sat across from him in the one free chair. In an attempt to help, his brain provided a comforting thought: a nice deep dark cave. *Wouldn't it feel good to crawl down into something like that, curl up on the ground facing the back wall, close your eyes, pull some moss over your body, sleep for a hundred years?*

He wasn't sure how much longer he could sit there. His father looked as if he was trying to find something to say.

"So, Dad, today I've got two classes to teach," Oscar lied. "But I'll be back right after. Do you think you'll be all right?"

Lee looked surprised. "Do you really think you can?"

"The semester's just getting started, is the thing." While he spoke, Oscar texted his best friend and nearest contemporary in the philosophy department, Sundeep, a fellow assistant professor:

Aren't you free Monday mornings? Squash in 30?

"I wouldn't want to abandon my students now," Oscar said. Sundeep responded in the affirmative immediately.

"In fact, I've got to get going or I'll be late."

Oscar went into his bedroom to change his shirt and put on shoes. He jammed his squash racquet into his backpack— half of the handle jutted out of the zipper. Thinking *am I really about to do this?* he took it back out, quietly opened the window, and dropped the racquet one half story into a bush below.

Back in the living room, his father was standing by the bookcase, head cocked sideways to read the spines. "Lots of Germans!" he said.

"Okay, I've got to run. Try not to...to think about things too much. There's food in the—well, actually the fridge is pretty empty but there are takeout menus, and I'll bring something home. And then we'll talk."

Outside, Oscar collected the racquet from the bush, unlocked and mounted his bike, and took off on a route to the school's athletic center that would minimize the chances of running into any of the students he'd canceled on. This was bad, surely, to be abandoning his father. Not only bad but in fact immoral. He could fully appreciate this fact. But then, it couldn't have been that bad if here he was, doing it.

The athletic center had a long line of gleaming squash courts, all empty at this hour. He met Sundeep at the court they preferred and they shook hands, in their tradition, before changing into their shorts and non-marking shoes. They dressed almost wordlessly, like men preparing to rob a bank, and stepped into the court through the little door in the glass wall.

Sundeep was the type of man whom Oscar might resent if he weren't also so likeable. He was two inches taller than Oscar, handsome and brilliant in the type of non-congenital way that required a tremendous academic work ethic. He was born to immigrant parents, both doctors, who had suffered to arrive and survive in America, and as such he had a boundless optimism for his own capabilities and, it seemed, zero self-doubt. He had already had three papers published, to relative acclaim in his niche of normative ethics, as opposed to Oscar's one published defense of compatibilism. Oscar envied him, how his intelligence seemed to be an extension of his deeper goodness, rather than an impediment to normal life.

Sundeep served to start their first game.

Oscar was nowhere near as talented at squash as Sundeep, but he loved the sport, how it asked for grace but would settle for fury. Through what he considered to be sheer willpower, he was able to win about a quarter of their games, or a third if he was particularly dialed in, which was enough of a chance to keep things interesting.

Sundeep's control of the ball was pure artistry; with an imperceptible flick of his wrist he could place it anywhere he pleased, in either a graceful arc that seemed almost to touch the ceiling or in a laser-beam line a centimeter from the sidewall. Oscar was a flat-footed brute by comparison, but every now and then he could line one up and blast it back into the corner with enough power to catch Sundeep out of rhythm.

They played for an hour and a half, the only conversation between them the occasional bellowed expletive that echoed through the empty courts.

Afterward, Oscar was completely soaked with sweat. He wrung his shirt out into a trash bin. Sundeep was only damp. Oscar had won five games out of eleven, which he was pleased with. In immediate retrospect, he appreciated that the exercise and competition had effectively obliterated his consciousness for a time and that he had spent the last little while apart from the concerns that now threatened to return.

"I'm slipping," Sundeep said.

"I should tell you something," Oscar said, still huffing for breath. "My mother died yesterday."

Sundeep stopped untying his shoe and stood up. "Dude... are you serious?"

Oscar explained the circumstances.

"Holy shit. I am so sorry. Just yesterday?"

"Yeah. It's very weird. I'm sorry."

"Don't say sorry. It's not weird. Not at all. Strange, yes, maybe. What are you going to do?"

"I don't know. My dad is at my place. That's actually why I needed your car. Oh—can I please have it for one more day?"

"Of course. He's there right now? Shouldn't you go back?"

"You're right. I...yes."

"You should go back, I think. In these times it's important to be with family."

"Definitely. Just needed to clear my head."

"Yeah. Well, listen—if there's anything I can do."

"Thank you."

"What was her name, so I can pray for her?"

"Delia."

Oscar took a long, scalding shower and then lay down on a bench in the locker room with a towel over his eyes. Endorphins still hummed pleasure into his muscles, but his mind had re-sharpened, and his thoughts once again cast themselves further into the future than the next few moments.

Through a vent, from some adjacent reality, he heard the pleasant sounds of the swim team hitting the pool, splashes and whistles and echoes.

He liked to consider and declare himself an enemy of cliché, but he found himself entirely constricted by it now. *She's gone!* he kept thinking. *Totally gone. And isn't that just so incredibly strange and sad.* He tried to come up with a more sophisticated way to express what he was feeling and could not.

Not only was she gone, but her impression of him that she had carried with her and refined since their first sublimely traumatic moment of his birth was gone, as well. This special appreciation of him had drifted off like a tendril of smoke into a dark night. It inhered nowhere. He felt diminished in a way that he knew would last forever.

But I suppose this is the way it goes, he thought. *You have a certain number of lights on inside you, lit when you're young, and little by little other people wink them out when they leave, and then when it's your time to go, if you're lucky, it feels perfectly appropriate.*

This was a dark, shitty, and dumb thought, he knew, but hey, why not—a certain quantity of self-pity seemed fair. He was too young for this loss, after all, by at least ten or fifteen years.

When he walked through the door of his apartment an hour later with a pathetically small and poorly considered bag of groceries, his father sat in one of the two living room chairs. It seemed as if perhaps he hadn't left the room.

"Hi, Dad."

"Oscar, will you come sit down? You were right, actually. There is something we should talk about."

3

"We had planned on your mother explaining this to you and now I'm not sure I know where to begin." Lee had his fingers interlaced and he looked down at the floor. Oscar sat down. "I suppose it's a long story but I don't think that I could maintain the thread from start to finish so let me just tell you here first that the money is gone."

"Wait. What money?" Oscar said. "Whose money?"

Before his retirement, Lee had owned a small business, started by his father, that sold and serviced dental supplies. Oscar's mother had taught public school for her entire career. There had been a few lean Christmases here and there, but they had always provided Oscar and his sister with a life that most would consider middle class, at least. To the best of Oscar's knowledge, his parents had made sound investments and rarely splurged. Their one major expenditure of the last decade had been the "home gym" they built in Oscar's room when he moved out, which consisted of a treadmill and a Nautilus weight machine that after six months saw almost zero use.

"Have you ever heard of Paul St. Germaine?" Lee said. "He's a philosopher just like you."

"Dad, what are you talking about? Did something happen to your money?"

"That's what I'm trying to tell you. This is not easy for me. Paul St. Germaine is a—well, I'm not sure what. A speaker type of guy. A thinker."

Oscar's imagination took over and immediately constructed a thousand terrible scenarios based on this foundation, a grand edifice of disaster with many halls yet to be explored. He gestured impatiently for his father to continue.

"We saw him first on the TV. He had a show on there that was all about the human mind and how to unlock its potential. It was your mother who started watching first, actually. She was going through some of her harder times then, and she liked what he had to say. There was only one show, an infomercial I suppose is what you'd call it, which was an hour long, but at the end a number comes up and you can send away for tapes."

"Tapes?"

"DVDs. So we ordered the DVDs and—"

"Wait. Dad. How bad is this?"

"Well, I'm trying to tell you."

"Dad."

There was a pause. Lee didn't look up. "Bad is not the word I would choose."

"How bad?"

"I've decided to look at it as a new beginning."

"I don't understand," Oscar said.

"Well, will you let me tell you?"

Oscar acquiesced with silence and tried to quiet his clattering mind. Lee picked up an empty mug that was on the table, looked at it, set it back down. He did not look at Oscar when he resumed speaking.

"We get the tapes in the mail, there's a whole bunch of boxes, and your mother just falls right into them. I mean, it only took her four or five days to watch them all. She wanted me to watch with her, naturally, but as you know I don't go in much for that kind of stuff. But I do notice that she starts to seem different. Happier. She was getting up in the morning without hitting the snooze.

"And then when she'd watched all the tapes—in fact I think she watched them all twice, maybe three times—she comes to me and tells me about these get-togethers that Mr. St. Germaine has, I guess you'd call them seminars or retreats, where you can go and meet other people who like him and like what he has to say on his tapes, and you all stay together in one big hotel, and he gives more lectures about your brain and how to control it."

Oscar rubbed his face with both hands.

"Dad...you do know what this sounds like, right?"

"Yes, yes, but no, it's not like that. He's a very smart man. I can't much follow a lot of what he talks about, but it's obvious he's a smart man."

"Does this story end with you writing a check to a cult leader?"

"Don't say that," Lee snapped. "It's not a cult. Really, it's not. And I know that's what someone would say if it was, but no."

"But you did?"

"Well, so, I figured since your mother responded so positively, we could afford to take out a bit of our savings and go to Hawaii to one of these retreats."

"Without telling me."

"You only would have tried to stop us. But Oscar, if you had been in the house and seen the state your mother was in when it was getting really bad—she wouldn't eat. Wouldn't come to the phone. For a long time, she wouldn't leave the house at all, and then there would be weeks where she would go to church twice a day. I begged her to see a doctor, anyone, but she refused. One night, she told me that she had thought about..." His voice caught. "That it was nearly too much for her to bear. It killed me, how powerless I was to help. And then suddenly, to see her change when she found Paul, it was incredible, like a miracle. A rebirth. You would have spent the money, too."

"I wish you had told us it was getting that bad."

"What would I have said? You're here at school. You would only worry."

"I had a right to know."

"She was a private woman."

Oscar seethed and said nothing.

"Point being, she showed so much improvement after the first time we went—"

"You went more than once? How many times?"

"Will you let me speak? She showed so much improvement that we decided to go again."

The conversation began to wind around itself, taking on the repetitive rhythm that can only occur in arguments between family members. It was ten more minutes before Lee got to the point, which was that, in addition to the cost of flights and expenses, there was a kind of retreat-within-the-retreat, available only to "students" with a certain level of experience, that this St. Germaine offered to those he deemed worthy. There was an additional fee for this admission, which was twenty thousand dollars. Lee had paid for his wife to attend four times.

"Twenty thousand!" Oscar nearly choked.

"Do you want me to say I feel like a fool? Well I won't, because I don't. That money bought your mother…" here his voice wavered and he collected himself "…bought your mother, the woman I loved more than life itself for forty-three years, a little peace, when she couldn't get it anywhere else."

They breathed through the first long silence since Lee had asked Oscar to sit, which indicated that something had occurred and concluded. They both slumped, not looking at each other. Oscar thought for a moment and then spoke, as the venom began to seep inward from the wound.

"Dad, so…you're broke. That's what this talk is."

"Please don't talk down to me about this."

"How can you tell me this so calmly? Are you not…mad at this guy?"

"He helped your mother. Quite a bit. It may have been costly but your mother's last days were her happiest. I don't care about myself as much."

"And Mom thought this was an okay thing to do, too? To

say nothing about what Gracie and I stood to inherit—what about the rest of your lives?"

"Oscar, I loved the woman. She was in pain. I don't think we did the wrong thing. We wanted to come and tell you about how much improvement there had been in her life and tell you about St. Germaine—a totally different conversation from the one we're having now. I am informing you, not apologizing to you."

In all of Oscar's life, they had never discussed Delia's depression so openly. They had in fact almost never used the word *depression*, just as they hadn't in this conversation. Throughout Oscar's childhood, it was understood that occasionally it would be necessary for Mom to stay in her room, in her bed, for two or three or four days. During this time, she would exist in a kind of half sleep, watching soap operas on the portable black-and-white set or reading paperback novels a slow page at a time. Lee explained to Oscar and his sister that sometimes their mother got very tired and had to rest and that she wasn't to be disturbed unless it was very important. Lee would bring in trays of food for her and bring them back out almost untouched. When enough time had passed, his mother would emerge from the darkness, scoop up the nearest child, and kiss them like she had returned from a long trip. This was simply part of the rhythm of life in the Boatwright household, a fact that Oscar had gradually grown into, which made it hardly notable.

It wasn't until years later that he realized that his mother's days spent behind closed blinds were so clearly a symptom of something, and that the defeated wryness of her humor and a certain melancholic suite of her mannerisms were surely vents from some deeper chamber of her being. It had taken Oscar finally thinking of his mother as a person and not just as his mother to come to this realization.

Oscar wasn't sure if he had inherited this depression. There were certainly periods of his life in which it seemed that the largest part of himself was dedicated to dread. He often looked at sleep as an escape rather than a necessity. Of course he often felt that his intelligence and sensitivity were burdens rather than gifts. And if he did sometimes fantasize about being dead, he never thought about killing himself, at least not seriously. But when things were going well, he felt generally good. So what if things were rarely going that well? Where does brain chemistry give way to logic?

"Oscar, I'll be honest. I'm scared to be alone. I need my son. I've been in this room all morning, thinking, what do I do now? I realize now that I may never have told you this plainly, it's such a simple thing. But I loved her so, so, so much."

Oscar dropped back down into the chair and let his air leave him in an exhausted sigh. What did he have to offer this man?

Lee continued, more talkative now than perhaps Oscar had ever seen him.

"There's something I keep remembering, from when we were young, your mother and I. We had only been married a month or two, and I got up early to go to work, and she would stay in bed for a little while. But this one time, as I stood there in the doorway looking at her, she got out of bed and held her head to my chest, just stood there holding me, and after she got back in bed I went into the other room and dropped down on my knees, you know that's not something I usually do, and thanked God for sending me this woman, which I really do believe that he did. It's hard to explain to you just what I was feeling but that's the memory that I have."

"It's okay, Dad. You don't have to explain to me. That's a very nice memory. You should keep remembering that."

"You know—there's one more thing. I've been looking around at your books. I was kind of hoping you might be able to give me some ways to stay...positive," Lee said. "You know, like some things that you've read. In your studies."

"Dad, we've talked about this. That's not really what philosophy is."

That night, after Lee had gone to bed, Oscar opened his laptop and Googled Paul St. Germaine. The first link was his personal website, which was of a primitive, outdated design and featured a close-cropped headshot set against a field of stars. He didn't look aggressively charismatic; he appeared to be in his fifties, graying hair, roundish face with slightly knobby features, and a wry smile. Below his photo, the text read "As seen on TV!" Clicking the tab marked Bio brought up only one sentence: "Pioneering thinker Paul St. Germaine has helped millions worldwide to lead happier and more productive lives through harnessing the power of their own minds." No real credentials could be ascertained.

The site was thin on content and appeared to exist mostly as a portal to buy the DVDs, which had to be purchased as a full set of fifteen, for the price of one-ninety-five (plus S&H).

Thinking that his family deserved at least this much, Oscar broke one of his minor moral codes, and after clicking around a bit, was soon illegally downloading the first of the fifteen installments. While he waited for the download to complete, he combed through more of the Google search results, which contained an odd absence of criticism about St. Germaine and his programs.

Oscar mostly found message board threads (hosted on websites like BuildABetterYou.com and TheExaminedLife.com) where people discussed, in the internet patois of the over-sixty set that featured abundant capitalization and exclamation points, whether they should invest in the DVDs. One user with a dancing fluffy pink avatar wrote, PAULS PROGRAM LITERALLY SAVED MY LIFE!!!! DON'T BE A CHEAPSKATE!!!! Just below that, another user wrote, This guy is a total con artist. Depressed? Save your money and get some sun and hit the gym.

Oscar could find almost no mention of the retreats, aside from one person who started a responseless thread with the title So who will I be meeting in Hawaii?

When the download was complete, he pressed Play and leaned back and crossed his arms over his chest.

After one second he hit Pause again. He got up and walked around the living room with his hands on his hips, tried to breathe deeply, heart rate elevated. Through the window over the sink he could see a fir tree illuminated by a streetlight. He went back to the computer and hit Play again.

The first image to appear was the title card of what must have been the production company, Samsara, accompanied by a few synthesized tones. The video quality was grainy and the audio lo-fi; it appeared to have been recorded sometime in the midnineties. This then faded into gold superimposed lettering that read "Session 1: An Introduction."

Slowly an image began to fade in from the black: St. Germaine sat cross-legged in a leather chair, with his hands folded over his knee, wearing a gray suit with a thin tie, smiling. Next to the chair was a blank whiteboard on an easel, and between the chair and the easel was a tall potted plant. All this was set up in the corner of a nondescript white room.

St. Germaine began to speak:

"Welcome, welcome, welcome. My name is Paul St. Germaine, and I couldn't be happier that we've found each other and that you've decided to embark with me on a journey of self-improvement."

His voice was warm and richly textured and Oscar was annoyed that he wasn't immediately able to hate him as much as he would have preferred.

"I can't see you through the screen, but I hope you'll forgive me if I make a few assumptions about you, based partly on statistical likelihood and partly on empirical observations that I've made over my career about the type of people who most often find their way to me: You are an American. You are safe. You are educated. You are guaranteed never to starve to death, and most of the dangerous elements of nature are of little or no concern to you. You live in a world far less violent than even as recently as when your parents were your age. You work hard but you generally don't have to worry about money. Or, if you do worry about money, it's about money for things like the lease on a second car and not for food or shelter. I bet you even have a family that loves you, and you love them right back. But why, then, are you so miserable?"

Oscar was caught off guard by the word choice. *Miserable? Who is this for?*

He hit Pause and stared at the face on the screen, with its

eyes closed as if right before a sneeze. The face that had talked his parents out of everything. He tried to imagine his mother seeing this for the first time, sitting in their television room, holding the remote to the DVD player that Oscar had set up for them. She was a smart woman, and nobody's mark. How could she see in this man a savior?

Oscar hit Play.

"Let me tell you a few more things about you," St. Germaine continued. "You are constructed out of matter that was born in the furnace-hearts of dying stars. This matter traveled on a billion-year adventure through many forms before composing itself into you, and then something breathed consciousness into your brain, and you were sent out into the world to do as you would. But you were never given a user's manual for your body, or your brain, which of course is part of your body. And sometimes things go wrong, just like with a car or refrigerator. And now here you are, with me, at the absolute cutting edge of time, broken and lost.

"Over the course of the fifteen lessons that you've purchased, we're going to write a new user's manual for our brains. We're going to learn all sorts of ways to coexist with our brain in peace. We're going to talk about a number of different techniques, but they mostly can be boiled down into these four main tenets:

1. We're going to learn to love our own insignificance.
2. We're going to learn to control our frame of reference.
3. We're going to remember to always consider the end.
4. Don't be scared, but we're going to reject free will entirely.

"It's not going to be easy to let go of much of what you have been taught. But if you can, if you're willing to follow along with me and truly consider what I aim to show you, then I promise that you can be set free."

Oscar closed the video. One side effect of his experience in academia was that he was incapable of hearing arguments or ideas without trying to pick them apart, and he was not currently in the proper state to shoulder this dreck.

He left his laptop open while it downloaded the rest of the videos.

Once he heard his father snoring through the thin walls, Oscar snuck out of the apartment, walking around the less creaky edge of the room like he was sixteen again, and got on his bike. His little neighborhood was dark and quiet, although he could hear the thumping bass from a party going on somewhere closer toward campus. He had no idea why he had come outside or where he was going. He picked a direction. Left.

He was almost thirty, his childhood was obviously over and had been for a long time, but what was ending now, and ending so terribly, felt to him like something close to childhood. He felt abandoned, although to say that his parents had abandoned him, his mother into death and his father into helplessness, seemed unfair. But then how to explain what he was feeling?

He biked into town, under the train trestle painted in the collegiate colors, down onto campus, around the science building and through the main quad on the paths that were best lit. It felt good to have the night air in his face, whistling through the gaps of his dorky helmet, his most important decision which way to turn at each crossroads.

As he biked faster and faster, he felt something open up inside of him, some old valve being loosened that he knew was only in his head although he perceived it as if the spout sat somewhere right above his stomach, sickly tar spilling down into his core like a busted pipe in the basement.

Part of the reason that Oscar didn't consider himself a depressive was that he had never read or seen a depiction of anything that reminded him of the particular way that he sometimes felt terrible. His manifestation of the thing that he didn't call depression didn't hover over him like a great black wing, didn't feel like falling through a void or staring into an abyss or any of the other clichés. All of these analogies seemed too large; there was nothing grandiose about his experience, nothing particularly dramatic. It didn't even seem like a matter of the largeness of a particular negative energy but rather a smallness.

Each cell of his body felt small and more distant from all of the other cells. His passions felt small. His capacity for love, both to give and to receive, felt small. His brilliant ideas felt small, even though they were correct; that was part of it, they were correct and perfect and still so small, so useless. Anything that bore any kind of meaning or substance for him would get smaller and smaller until it threatened to be sucked into itself like a snake eating all of its own tail and then finally successfully eating the head and mouth that's doing the eating, and winking out of existence. Was this depression? *Probably, dummy,* he thought.

He was flying too fast through the darkness from each island of yellow light produced by the sodium poles to the next, lactic acid building up in his thighs, his lungs straining for air, eyes watering against the wind.

On his way back, he biked past the party where the noise was coming from, an off-campus wreck of a house with a wraparound porch that was currently overflowing with students congregated around what looked to be at least three kegs. As he approached, slowly now, regaining his wind, he saw a student hop over the railing of the porch, jog down to a gray car that was idling at the curb, and get in the passenger seat. By the dome light, he saw that the kid had money in his hand and was holding it up to the figure behind the wheel. The hand was quickly pushed down, out of sight.

Oscar took a moment to look back once he had coasted past. The student placed something small into his shirt pocket and gave an emphatic double thumbs-up to his friends waiting for him back on the porch. A cheer went up.

4

"Another plane," Lee said.

"It's not a long flight, Dad. Gracie will meet you when you land and take you home."

They stood outside of security where only two days ago they had met, where the new epoch of Oscar's life had dawned. The airline had already transported the remains back to Indiana, which was something that Oscar had never really thought about—dead bodies transported via air—but of course it happened all the time. She, her body, was waiting for them at one of the two funeral homes in town, where she had in fact seen both of her own parents laid out and visited by their few loved ones.

"And I'll be seeing you soon, yes? You're not going to miss your own mother's funeral? Will you tell me when you've gotten your ticket?"

"The airline said that they will bump someone for me if need be. Of course I'll be there."

Lee looked at his watch. Oscar expected that now he would say something that passed for goodbye and head over to stand in line, but he remained where he was, and Oscar realized that his father felt the need for something more.

"There's a lot more we should talk about," Oscar said. "I'm sorry. I consider that my fault. But I'll be home soon and we can fix that."

"Okay, Oscar. That sounds like a plan."

Oscar looked into his father's face and was nearly overcome with all that he saw there. Age, pain, regret, loneliness, and of course himself, Oscar, in the line of the jaw and the way that the eyes were set back from the nose. A vision of the future.

"Oscar, your mother—you know how much she loved you, don't you?"

"Yes, Dad."

"I love you that much, too."

"I love you too, Dad."

The two men hugged, firmly but briefly, and then Lee turned and walked toward his plane.

5

Oscar returned to campus, finalized his travel arrangements, did some grading, and went to bed. The next day he taught his classes, packed a duffel bag into which he jammed his one dark blue suit, and had Sundeep drop him off back at the airport in the evening for his flight.

When the flight attendant came over the PA to announce that electronic devices could now be turned on, Oscar opened his laptop and booted it up. He plugged in his headphones, angled the screen slightly toward the window after the woman sitting next to him peeked sidelong over her nose, and opened the file named PSGvol2.

The audio came up to a fuzzy neutral, like the first few seconds after a needle is lowered onto a vinyl album, and then the Samsara title card appeared accompanied by synthesized tones, and then text that read "Session 2: Foundations." And then there was St. Germaine, the same room, the same potted plant, the same whiteboard, even the same suit. Oscar felt his heart rate quicken, his upper lip curl slightly.

"Welcome again! You've made one of the biggest steps, which is of course deciding to come back, so congratulations. Are you watching this tape immediately after the previous one? If so, I'm flattered, but remember that I recommend that you allow at least a few days between sessions, in order to let what we've spoken about sink in. This will become especially important down the road, when I ask you to implement some practical aspects into your day-to-day lives."

St. Germaine shifted his head and the video cut to another camera only slightly to the left of the first one. The view of the whiteboard and the plant barely shifted at all, but from the new angle, St. Germaine looked like a different man entirely.

"When last we spoke, I laid out our goals, and a bit of the framework as to how we're going to achieve them. Today I'd like to build on that framework and get us underway. So, shall we?"

He raised a knuckle to his lips in a moment of thought before he began.

"There was something I said last time that might have alarmed you, and that was about the matter of free will. Now, I know that this is an issue with religious implications for many people, and since I don't claim to be a theologian, I certainly don't wish to step on anyone's toes in that arena, but maybe you'll allow me to ask you a few questions? Feel free to pause the tape at any point if you'd like."

He got up and uncapped a dry-erase marker that lay on the metal lip of the whiteboard. With a neat hand, he wrote:
1. Define.

"I wonder, can you tell me what free will actually *is*? Not a definition, i.e., the ability to act without the constraint of fate or necessity, but rather describe it as a phenomenon?

"Let me give you a few examples of descriptions of other abstract ideas, to show how I think free will is a unique case.

I would describe *love* in simple and perhaps imprecise terms, as a profound sense of goodwill toward and connectedness with someone. I would describe *the soul* as that part of us which contains our feelings and undergoes perception. But what *is* free will itself?

"Both love and the soul are famously elusive and amorphous ideas, but nonetheless we can at least arrive at workable definitions with relative ease. Can we do the same for free will? Is it just some undetectable force that exists entirely outside the influence of any other force? Perhaps you'd like to say that it's merely some kind of indescribable state of things that we hope is the case and not a thing itself, but that doesn't seem to help much and probably only weakens the argument for its existence.

"Maybe you did come up with something. But I know that, for my part, I've never heard a satisfying definition. Is this a deathblow for the general conception of free will? Of course not. But it's a point against, I think."

Next he wrote:

2. *Imagine.*

"Take a moment to imagine your life if the free will that you assume you possess was removed from you. You would still make decisions just like usual, only it would be the case, unbeknownst to you, that you could have never chosen otherwise. In what way is this life different from the one you're leading now? Is it different at all?

"And finally—" He picked up the pen and wrote:

3. *Decide.*

"Is either case preferable to you? Why?"

St. Germaine capped the marker and went back to his chair. The camera angle changed again.

"Now, I'm very sympathetic to what I'm sure you're feel-

ing right now, which is most likely some slight alarm or discomfort, the need to push back, maybe even a bit of anger at
me. After all, if we don't possess this thing called free will,
then every time you've made a moral decision, you actually
have nothing to feel good about, as you don't deserve credit
for that which you couldn't have avoided doing. (I actually
don't think that that's the case, but we'll get more into that
later.) And of course, the flip side, which is somewhat less
offensive to our ego, is that you also don't deserve blame for
the bad things that you do.

"Why does this matter, you're asking? How does this bear
at all on what you're feeling? I'll tell you why."

Here a look came over St. Germaine's face, a submerged
quality rising to just below the surface. He paused for a moment to glimmer at the camera before continuing.

"Because the way you feel has so much to do with thoughts
of who and what you are. How useless, how superfluous, how
broken, how dumb. How you could have done things differently, led a different life. Because you still think that you are
you. But you are not you. You are a collection of impulses
currently moving through the same location that that which
you call 'you' also happens to currently inhabit."

He took a sip from a clear plastic cup of water that he kept
out of frame. An odd editorial choice, Oscar thought.

"I know some of the language I've been using might be a
little confusing at first, but please rewind the tape if you've
had trouble keeping up. This will all be very important later.

"All I ask is that you follow me a bit further."

6

Oscar's sister had offered to pick him up from the airport, but he decided to rent a car, mostly to provide himself with the illusion of freedom and the possibility of escape. He picked up the car, a black sedan, and in a few minutes, he was cutting through the big-sky expanse of his native land.

So many artists had been inspired by the quintessentially American melancholy of the Midwest, but as a young man Oscar had found the landscape oppressive in its openness. The plains, to Oscar, seemed to impose a logic of their own, something akin to the maddening contemplation of the infinite, or the way the ear strains to the point of hallucination in a perfectly quiet room, desperate to detect a sound.

After an hour's drive from the airport and a brief detour past his old high school to see if it had changed (it hadn't), he came to the house. It was low and long like a wall at the top of a rise, a yellow postwar ranch that had faded with time into the color of broth. He had been back here once in the last three years, when his parents bought him a flight to come for Christmas. He parked in front of the garage alongside a white BMW that he couldn't place, until he remembered his sister saying something about a new car.

This was all cast in a feeling of complete unreality until he stepped out of the car and felt the crunch of the old gravel under his boots and smelled the lilacs that his mother had planted in the side garden. Something inside of him reverted to a former state. He had come home.

He entered without knocking, and his sister heard him from the kitchen, where a pot was simmering on the stove.

"Look at this guy," she said as she pulled oven mitts off of her hands. They hugged. He didn't realize until he was embracing her how much he had missed her.

"Where's the old man?" Oscar said, looking around. There were paper plates, cups, and pizza boxes strewn about the surfaces of the room. Photos of his mother had been arranged on the dining room in a semicircle around a candle, which had gone out. He picked them up. Here she was on horseback as a child, here she was holding a diploma and smiling, here she was in her wedding dress, here she was holding baby Oscar at some fairground, with one hand up to shield the sun from her eyes, shadow over her face.

"Some of the Knights of Columbus guys took him out for a beer. You missed the action by a few hours. Some teachers from Mom's school. A few kids from her class. The Andersons."

The Boatwrights had very little family; Lee had lost his older brother to Vietnam, and there was a sister that he never spoke to or mentioned who lived in Oregon. Delia Boatwright was an only child. There had been distant grandparents in small homes far away, and then hospitals, but no longer.

"Let's sit though. My little brother's home!"

They sat down on the high-backed couch. Oscar slung a slice of cold pizza onto a paper plate.

"We've barely talked. How are you handling it?" she said. "You've caught me at a moment when my tear tanks are empty, but don't let me fool you, I'm a wreck."

"Where are the kids?"

"With John, at the movies."

Grace's three pregnancies had done nothing to diminish her beauty. She had stayed with the Midwest and the Midwest had stayed with her, in her sandy hair and freckles and features made for gazing at a distant horizon, in the set of her jaw and the way she kept one bent wrist to her hip when she stood.

"I don't know," Oscar said. "It's tough to say what's normal, right? Assuming that a mother's death is one of the hardest things you've got to go though, then I'm probably doing just about normal, given that I feel run-over, panicky, and a brand-new type of alone, when I allow myself to feel anything at all."

Gracie made a face. It did not matter that Oscar had been bad about returning her calls. She knew him too well.

"Oh, Oscar. You can just say you're sad, and I can hug you, like this."

She came across the couch and hugged him again. This was something she had picked up somewhere, this ease with physical affection and comfort, and Oscar was glad that it had made a foothold in their family, even if he wasn't quite as receptive to it as he wished he could be.

He spoke into her shoulder, hugging her back around her rib cage. "I can't believe she's gone. Isn't that crazy?"

"Totally."

"This blows!"

"Yeah. I already miss her so much."

They stayed like this. Oscar tried to disengage, but she held firm, and he recommitted.

Oscar had always been bad at talking to his sister. It wasn't that he didn't want to connect with her, but a four-year age difference meant that he had always looked up to her too much to ever really consider her a true peer. Most of his memories of her were images of idol worship: a crack shot with their father's .22 (and later, the .308) when Oscar was still upset by the recoil, an excellent student when Oscar was still frustrated by his inability to memorize his times tables, starting point guard on the girl's basketball team when Oscar's body was still thin and undeveloped. And then by the time he hit high school, she had already moved out, decamping on a bus to New York City the morning after a titanic fight with their father over some trivial issue that had been lost to time, taking with her the money that she had saved from working in a frozen yogurt store.

In New York she found work as a waitress and a dog walker. She lived in the East Village and dated a series of bohemian men whose art projects and punk bands she would describe to Oscar in emails and clandestine phone calls. Her parents gave her more space than either she or Oscar had expected, either out of resignation or (he had hoped) a more parentally skillful maneuver of letting her work out a year of wanderlust in the hopes that she would return home and go to college, preferably somewhere close by.

But she was still on the east coast five years later when Oscar, in his own watered-down version of rebellion, went off to a fancy liberal arts college in western Massachusetts, rather than the nearby state university. This "rebellion" was of course rebellion in name only, and in fact not even in name but only in Oscar's head, as it was funded by the very monarchs who were being rebelled against and who made much less issue than they had right to of the fact that it would cost them about four times as much to send their child off a thousand miles to a town so liberal that it seemed at times like a cautionary tale in a right-wing chain letter. (It had been rumored that the chamber of commerce had in fact once issued a letter to Strategic Command informing them that in the case of a nuclear exchange with the Soviet Union, American missiles were not permitted to use the town's airspace.)

Oscar realized now that on some level he had wanted to follow his sister, even if he only made it to the same coast.

He went to visit her during fall break of his freshman year of college. Her apartment, a studio over a tattoo parlor, was so jammed with books and hookahs and her friends' surprisingly good art that it seemed as if she had lived an entirely new, full life in the last five years. They ate dinner standing up in the kitchen of a Turkish restaurant where she knew the cook and went to a punk show on the Bowery to see a local band she liked. (A year later, they were famous.) Then they got drunk on cheap beers at a bar where one of the few things he remembered was one of her friends, a beautiful girl in a purple leather jacket, throwing her arm around his shoulder and asking, "Is this the little Boat?" and that when he tried to kiss her later that night, her refusal was totally cool and not damaging to his ego in the least. When he and his sister finally stumbled home, the sun was coming up over the East River.

It was one of the most fun nights of his life, but deep down he felt a bit like a fringe member of a rock star's entourage. This was not to say that Gracie treated him brusquely; in fact she was delighted to see him and include him in her life after so much time apart. It was just that her life was so cool, so underpinned with a bold recklessness that was entirely inaccessible to him, how could he ever be a substantial part of it?

That would be the first and last time he ever got to visit her in New York. In the spring, for reasons that she never fully made clear to him, she finally did what her parents had assumed she would do, only four years late: she went home. She dumped the graphic designer she was seeing, sold off everything that was too large to fit into her two duffel bags, got back on the bus, and for the first time, went home. She got an apartment a few miles from her parents and a job as a receptionist in a real estate office, but wasn't there for more than a year before she was engaged to John, whom she met while he was angling to buy a plot of land on which to build a strip mall, and they started having kids. That was nine years ago.

Oscar knew that it was wrong, unfair, and a little mean for him to think that her return from New York had made her life smaller or less meaningful. But for some reason her homecoming had disappointed him. Now when Oscar thought about her life, he was filled with sadness that he did not endorse, because to do so would imply that the life she could have lived, a life filled with loudness and color and invigorat-

ing danger, would somehow be preferable to the life of prai-
rie home companionship that she was living now, which he
was not ready to admit.

"If you can believe it, there's actually another shitty thing
we need to talk about," Oscar said.

"Oh?" Gracie said.

Oscar's shoulders slumped down into the couch. He hesitated to begin. "I hate how sure I am that Dad didn't tell you
anything about this."

"Oh yeah, the frigging Hawaii thing? Let's talk about this.
They just told me they wanted to take more vacation."

"Well, not quite."

Oscar explained to her, clearly but as quickly as he could
in order to get it over with, how their parents had given basically all of their money, over a series of secret trips across
the Pacific, to a self-anointed guru who specialized in some
sort of quasi-philosophical apologism that Oscar was still trying to figure out.

As he spoke, he saw the news begin to settle into her face,
and he looked away. When he was done, her eyes were wet,
and she looked stunned, but also something further.

"Oscar, I... I guess I don't know how to react. A guru?
And hold on, when you say *all* their money..."

"I'm pretty sure I mean it. I have no idea what Dad's going
to do," Oscar said. "Not to pry, but is John seeing any income
from that apartment development yet?"

Gracie stood up and went back to the kitchen. When Oscar
followed her, she was standing at the sink with her back to
him, wringing a dry dish towel in her hands. After a moment
she set it on the counter in a puddle of soapy water.

"Ah…" Her voice wavered, almost like a laugh. "I was hoping to not tell you this until later. I guess I need to admit to myself that it's true. But John and I—we—things have gotten…well, things are not great. I mean, it's very bad. Over, really." Gracie worried at the cross around her neck. "It started with the crash. All these properties just went straight to shit. We started fighting. I should have told you."

She was crying now.

"I'm so sorry to hear this," Oscar said.

"I wish I didn't have to tell you under these circumstances!" she cry-laughed.

"Are you going to be okay?" He went to her, didn't hug her, but stood near.

"These things happen," she said, wiping away a thin tear with the heel of her hand. She hiccuped once, something a bit like a sob. "We were so happy! We were so damn happy at the start you wouldn't believe it. I can still remember what it felt like. And then somehow things changed, and I hid from it, and it grew in the darkness and then one day I wake up and look around and I just go, oh my God, no, how can this be my life?"

Oscar put a hand on her back, avoided her eyes. "Gracie, it's not—I have faith we can come out of this all right."

"It's okay. I'll live. The kids will live, too, although I'm so worried about them. It's just that I had allowed myself to hope that I might be getting some help with maybe at least the legal bills."

Oscar found that all he could say was "I'm so sorry." He said it a few times.

7

The funeral took place in the church in which Oscar had been baptized. John and Grace sat with their three kids in between them. Oscar had shaken John's hand and, after an exchange of condolences, talked about baseball as if he knew nothing about the divorce grinding its way to finality.

The church was almost half-filled, which Oscar was glad to see, given the lack of extant Boatwrights. One row was occupied by the high school English department, and another with Mrs. Boatwright's students, the boys in ill-fitting suits, the girls in sundresses and black flip-flops, trying to keep it together under the dual stresses of the death of a maternal figure and the shattering of their specific reality. Your teacher doesn't *die*. Your grandmother dies.

Lee sat next to Oscar in his dark suit. On Lee's other side were men from the Knights of Columbus, an organization that contained the entirety of Lee's friends, and their wives. Oscar remembered most of these men from his youth, smoking cigarettes at backyard barbecues and complaining about the demands of their particular trade.

Oscar hadn't been sure if his sister's children, ages eight, seven, and five, were old enough to appreciate the gravity of what was going on, but now he was shamed with the obviousness of his answer—they bawled, gripping each other and the arms of their parents. They had loved their grandmother, who doted on them and made sure they knew that she loved them. Oscar, sitting behind them, rubbed their backs and shoulders, leaned over to wipe their running noses with Kleenex, and told himself he was going to be more present in their lives going forward.

At one point Lee got up and read a passage selected for him by the priest. Oscar read a selection as well, peering up only twice through the scrim of exhausted sadness that had settled over his eyes to look at the people assembled. In order to deliver the words without blubbering, he spent the first half of the mass cranking his emotions down into a smaller and smaller area that he felt behind his sternum and attempting to completely ignore what was going on. Much later, lying on his father's couch trying to get to sleep, Oscar would realize with aching regret that he had done too well at this and that he had not cried at all.

Toward the end of the proceedings, Lee went back up to speak. His remarks were so brief that it appeared as if he had decided at the last minute to edit and condense something longer that he had wished to say.

"My wife—" he said, his voice breaking up slightly and then reforming "—Delia, who I loved very much, felt the world too fully. It hurt her for a long time, and then it killed her. Amen."

Too short to be called a eulogy.

Oscar caught the priest, a man whom the Boatwrights had known for years, glance up at Lee with a look of annoyance, perhaps for the errant "amen," perhaps for the inglorious sentiment.

A special piece of religious cloth was arranged over the casket, and the priest sprinkled it with holy water. At the proper time, Oscar, along with his father, John, two Knights, and two men from the funeral parlor, took hold of the casket and walked it down the aisle to the waiting hearse. A sad hymn was played, which Oscar recalled from the past although he could not remember the words.

Later, at the gravesite, Oscar felt that under the cover of the melodrama it would be appropriate to talk about large things that otherwise might go unspoken for another decade.

"Can I ask you something?" he said to Gracie, who stood next to him with her children on her other side, as they all watched the shiny black casket lower into the dirty maw. His sequestered sadness had begun to return to him in a trickle, but he wished he could gather it all at once, because *here* was the time to really feel something, to have a good cry, instead of alone in an airplane bathroom on the way back west, but he supposed you didn't get to choose these things.

His sister gave him a look as if to say, now?

"I never figured it out. Why did you leave New York? What made you come back?"

Grace smiled with half her mouth. She nodded toward the direction of the casket. "She told me that once you moved out, she couldn't bear being alone. She said it was killing her to have none of her children around. I believed her."

8

Oscar is five years old. He can reach the top shelf of the refrigerator, but only if he stands on the vegetable drawer, which he has been told repeatedly not to do. His is a world of eye-level doorknobs and unseen countertops and furniture that he can fit his body under entirely, like the couch, which, when he is under it, feels like his own personal cave, among the coins and paperclips and forgotten toy cars like lost treasure.

It is late August, although he doesn't need or care to know this; summer vacation, his first, has been going on for so long that it's hard to recall the person he was when it began. He knows what letters are but can't yet read, and when his parents speak to each other using only letters, he knows that they are discussing something that he is not meant to understand. When outside of the house, he navigates the world attached to the hand of an adult, his arm bending upward as if holding an umbrella, but today he is home and there are no adults around. Oscar's sister is in the basement watching TV. His father is out working. His mother is in her room.

Oscar loves his mother very much and wants to make her happy. She is tired, and so she is resting, and has in fact been resting for two days. When Oscar is tired from too much play, he likes to have a snack, which gives him the energy to go back out and play some more, and so he decides that he will bring his mother a snack. Bringing her a snack will have the added effect of proving that he is no longer a baby and can be trusted with more difficult tasks, like for starters that he should be allowed to drink from glasses instead of plastic cups at the dinner table.

But he is smart enough not to overreach. He knows that he can't cook, and so after a quick perusal of the pantry, he decides that he will bring his mother a bowl of cereal, Honey Nut Cheerios specifically, a personal favorite of his. The combination of the discrete elements of bowl, spoon, Cheerios, and milk represents a medium level of difficulty, harder than a Jello Snack Pack and easier than anything involving heat, but he is up to the task.

And lo! An auspicious start! A bowl is already down from the cupboard. In fact it is the same bowl that Oscar himself had as recently as three hours ago eaten Honey Nut Cheerios out of, and therefore doesn't need washing. He goes into the drawer to get his mother a spoon, as the spoon that is currently sticking out of the bowl is a Ghostbusters spoon with a picture of Slimer on the handle, which is only for kids, and in fact only for Oscar.

He has to go up on his tiptoes to get down the box of Honey Nut Cheerios, and the box falls off the shelf and onto the kitchen floor, but it doesn't spill. He opens the tab on the box and unfurls the plastic bag within and then begins to pour, but never having done it before, he is not sure of the proper amount, and so he pours until cereal is level with the top of the bowl, which seems reasonable.

Happy with how easy this is proving, he opens the fridge, stands up on the vegetable drawer, and reaches up for the jug of milk, but he is surprised by its weight, which seems entirely unbelievable considering that his father can open and pour it with one hand while reading the paper with the other, and the jug plunges down and glugs itself empty onto the linoleum, while Oscar stands and watches from his perch.

This is bad, Oscar thinks, but not bad enough to entirely derail the original mission. He can still bring his mother the snack and come back to clean up the mess long before anyone finds out.

He considers salvaging some of the milk from the puddle on the floor but decides that there won't be enough. He considers just bringing her a bowl of dry cereal, but that seems silly, and so he decides to use water instead, which he knows is a bit unorthodox (he has never had his cereal with water) but at least better than dry, logically speaking. He opens the cold faucet and checks with his finger that it is at least as cold as the milk would have been, and then fills the bowl until a few Cheerios float off into the sink.

Slowly he begins the walk out of the kitchen, across the dining and living rooms, and up the stairs to his parents' room. He watches the bowl with monkish focus, making sure not to jostle it. He doesn't spill a drop.

He stands at the end of the hall before his parents' door,

which is slightly ajar. Here, in a mote-filled stream of sun-light, stands Oscar at the real moment of bravery. He knows that he is not to disturb his mother when she is resting. This is a very important rule. He steels himself. It is worth it. He knocks on the door with his foot. He hears nothing. She is probably sleeping. He pushes through.

The room is small and dark. The shades are drawn. The air conditioner hums. It's freezing in here. The small TV is on the nightstand facing in toward the queen-size bed, where his mother lies curled up on her side under the covers in the shape of a capital G. Oscar's will begins to falter. He shouldn't wake her up. He considers leaving.

But then her eyes open. She seems surprised to see him but not upset. She sits up in bed.

"Oscar...hi, honey," she says.

"Hi," Oscar says.

He still holds the bowl out in front of him. She moves over and makes a space for him to sit on the edge of the bed.

"Is this for me?" she says. Her black hair is tied back in a bun. She wears an oversized T-shirt emblazoned with Mickey Mouse. There is a smell in the room, something not unpleas-ant, something very human.

"I made it for you," he says. He hands her the bowl.

She lifts the spoon, tilts the surface of the bowl into the light.

"Is this... Did you try to get down the milk?"

Oscar had failed to realize that the lack of milk would raise questions. He panics a little but recovers himself.

"We were out of milk," he says.

"So you used water?"

"Is that wrong?"

"No, honey. That's very sweet."

"It's not bad?"

"No, it's fine. Here, look." She spoons some of the cereal into her mouth. She chews and swallows.

"It's delicious, bunny. Thank you," she says.

Oscar swells with pride. In his eyes she is elemental, enormous. As he sits and watches, she eats the entire bowl.

"Mom?" he says.

"Yes?"

"Nothing."

Thirty seconds pass.

"Mom?"

"Yes, Oscar?"

"I spilled the milk."

She laughs. Something has changed in her face.

"What do you say we go clean it up before your father gets home?" she says, and swings her legs out over the floor.

9

The air within the Boatwrights' house hung leaden with an unsettling finality. The stillness, hovering around the grandfather clock and the empty candy dish and small porcelain ballerina figurines in their glass case, indicated that although something bad had happened, it had now been taken care of, and all that remained to be done was break down the pizza boxes and tidy up the kitchen. There may have been one less of them, but those who remained were now free to go about their business, as all legal, religious, and societal requirements had been fulfilled.

At first the three Boatwrights had sat down in the living room, but Grace sensed almost immediately that she wanted no part of, or wouldn't be able to bear, the impending conversation, and so she had moved into the kitchen, where she began to very slowly wash the dishes.

"So," Oscar said to Lee, "it's time. We need to address the issue that's simplest to address, which is the financial one."

"What am I supposed to say?" Lee asked. "That I'm broke? Well, I'm broke."

"I'm just trying to look at the facts so we know what we're dealing with."

"Well, the facts are that I have very little—I can see out to the horizon about three months from now and beyond that I've chosen not to look."

"Dad—this is not like you."

"Well, it's like me now."

"*Well*, we still need a plan. I mean, come on! You own the house—you could sell it."

"I've lived in this house for forty-one years and here's where I'll die. Besides, have you looked at what's happened to property values?"

"We're talking about survival here."

"I know."

Oscar fought through the wrongness of all of this. His insides wrenched. This man had cared for him, clothed him, disciplined him, and now Oscar was putting him through this? But it had to be done.

"I guess let's focus on the numbers. I'll assume that the number in the bank is essentially zero."

"I have a few thousand or so left. The school gave me a nice check, too, to help with funeral expenses, almost another thousand. Plus there's your mother's life insurance, although much of that will go to the funeral home. There are probably a few things around the house that I could sell. I heard that that's easier these days, with the internet? I can live off my checks from the government, and maybe I can try to go back to work to see if I can pay off a little of the debt."

"Wait—what debt?"

A look came over Lee's face—he had let something slip, and he was ashamed about it, ashamed about the thing itself but almost more ashamed that his mind and memory were frayed enough to not do a better job of keeping it in.

"Wha—no. Don't tell me you *owe* this fucking St. Germaine guy? You *owe* him? How much?"

"I wasn't actually aware of this debt. I was never really involved. Your mother didn't tell—"

"How much?"

"Twenty-one thousand."

Oscar stood up suddenly. The hardback chair he was sitting on fell over backward with a bang. He bent to retrieve it while he started raising his voice.

"I can't believe what I'm hearing. Isn't this guy supposed to *help* people? How is it helping them to take all of their money and then invoice them for more? He wants to help people out of depression, or whatever? Well, aren't they going to be pretty depressed once they're bankrupt?"

"I don't know as much about the whole thing as you think I do. I took flights to Hawaii and stayed in the hotel and went to the beach while your mother went to the seminars. When she came back, she wouldn't talk about what went on, even when I pressed her."

"And yet you still wrote the checks."

"I thought you wanted the facts. You're lecturing me now."

Oscar exhaled and rubbed his forehead. "You're right. I'm sorry. So, okay, you owe the great and powerful holy man—"

"Oscar—"

"—twenty-one thousand dollars. And then, if we can get that taken care of, will you be okay?"

"Okay?"

In Lee's wrinkled face Oscar could see the widening of the man's perception of the rest of his life. Oscar tried to step in before he reached any sort of conclusion.

"Well, I mean in the sense of you won't starve or freeze."

"In that sense, yes, then I suppose I'll be okay. But Oscar, I'm your father, I'm not asking for any sort of—"

"Dad, we're past that, please, all right? We're past that. But I don't think you have to worry about taking any handouts just yet, because I've got nothing to hand out, and I don't think Gracie does either."

There was a silence.

"Dad, I'm—I'm sorry I raised my voice there for a second. I just can't see why you're not more alarmed."

"This is difficult to explain but I want to try." Lee looked exhausted, his eyes unfocused. "Eventually it just becomes hard to care. I've become…bored with this all. With being in this body. The thing that kept me going—I buried her today. I'm in a tough spot now, and I don't know what's going to happen to me. But right now, it's extremely hard to care. About money, especially. All my life I've had to worry about this—this filthy shit. I'm ready to be done with it."

Lee pulled his battered leather wallet out of his pocket and tossed it onto the table dismissively.

"First of all, Dad, you're not that old," Oscar said.

"Maybe not. But we're in the fourth quarter."

"And second of all—" Oscar paused to collect himself. "I didn't think this was ever going to be something that I would need to ask you, with Mom I thought maybe, but never you, so please don't be embarrassed, but if you ever think about—if you ever think you might be a danger to yourself, you need to call me immediately."

Lee made a derisive sound and dismissed the notion with a flap of his hand.

"Dad, I need you to please just promise."

"I promise."

Oscar stood up. He left his father and went to the kitchen (his sister was gone) and filled a glass of water from the tap. At the edge of the sink sat a spoon in a teacup on a saucer, and he had a thought about how these things were merely a temporary arrangement of molecules. Tip them over and they would fall apart and shatter.

Behind him, Lee stood up and slowly climbed the stairs to the second floor. His tread on the floor above him was different than Oscar remembered it—his footfalls whispered and dragged.

Oscar went to the broom closet where his father kept the rifles, and there they were, leaning barrels-up against the back corner, behind an ironing board. For a moment, he wondered if he should bury them in the woods behind the house, but then closed the closet door.

Oscar could feel a great force amassing itself outside his city walls, just beyond his perception, and for an instant he was able to appreciate the inevitability of his own destruction, truly understood it with a loving acceptance, but then it was gone.

His flight was scheduled to take off in three hours.

10

"Objects exist because they exist. This is good enough for our purposes. Things are the way they are because that's the way that they are. Events happen because they were always going to happen. You make the only decisions you can make. You are the only person you can be. You are the only person you can be. You are the only person you can be. Repeat that to yourself. Now once more. Again."

11

After the cheap midnight flight and a long cab ride back from the airport, Oscar got to the university as the sun was rising on Friday morning. He slept for two hours and woke to teach his intro section.

Afterward, he had a three-hour break before the start of his second class, and he planned to spend it in his favorite third-floor alcove in the library, studying the most impenetrable text he could get his hands on.

As he was walking up the library steps, Sundeep came out from inside.

"Hey, man. You're back already?"

"Long enough," Oscar said.

"Yeah. Yeah. Listen—how are you?"

Oscar tipped his head sideways back and forth. "Eh."

"Right. Well, look, I don't know if you've been keeping up with the bulletins but there's that guest lecturer in from Stanford to speak this evening, a Kantian I think? The paper is pretty good. Anyway I'm supposed to take him out for dinner afterward. Please come?"

Oscar knew that what he really wanted to do that evening, and for every evening following that he could currently foresee, was wallow in darkness. He knew that Sundeep probably knew this, as well.

"I don't know that I could be very interesting..."

"You don't have to be interesting, you just have to make me look smart. Come on. Please. See you tonight."

The philosopher was tall and stately in his late middle age, with a white beard and a prodigious stomach that strained the buttons of his dark double-breasted suit. He carried a brass-handled cane, which he kept in his hand at the podium while he enthusiastically delivered his talk to a lecture hall that contained nearly as many professors as students.

Sundeep had planned to bring the philosopher, along with Oscar and a few other professors in related areas of inquiry, to a nearby Italian restaurant, but the philosopher insisted on going to a bar instead, "somewhere with food," so that the half-dozen graduate students whom he had immediately befriended while lingering in the lecture hall could be invited.

The philosopher turned out to be far more game than most of the department's guest speakers and was soon avuncularly drunk on gin and tonics. He bought several rounds of drinks for everyone in attendance and outright refused to discuss the paper he had presented, which had been quite brilliant. After he handed Oscar his third bourbon on the rocks over Oscar's initial protestations, he threw his arm around his neck and said, "And what's your story, fellow? How goes the life of the mind?"

It felt good to be getting drunk, and he wondered why he hadn't done it sooner. It softened the edges of everything so that he could bump around safely. Feeling truthful, he replied, "I think it's killing me. And I'm so poor!"

"This is natural, dear boy, perfectly natural." His breath smelled like a juniper bush. "One must simply push through."

"For how long?"

"Oh, years and years, of course."

Sometime later, after another drink or maybe two, Sundeep spoke into Oscar's ear over the music.

"I think he'll be all right," he said, as the philosopher belted out a Rolling Stones song with a pair of townies. "Let's get out of here. I need to eat something other than fries."

The sun had not yet fully set. They went to the Italian restaurant, a few blocks away, just the two of them.

"Let me ask you something," Oscar said as the bottle of wine that Sundeep had ordered was uncorked, "have you ever heard of a guy named Paul St. Germaine?"

"Hmm. No? Who is he?"

"I'm not sure, exactly. Sort of like a motivational speaker. Considers himself something more. But anyway—my parents gave him all of their money." Oscar was slumped languidly in the booth. He lifted his wine up and toasted to nothing.

"Ah—Christ. All of it? Can anything be done?"

"Nothing has occurred to me. I can barely find any info about him."

Sundeep shook his head. "Man, you have truly been shat upon."

"Friend, I'll tell you," Oscar said with a laugh, sloshing wine into his mouth, "it's really something!"

Their food came out. Oscar had forgotten what he had ordered and was happy to see it.

Afterward, out on the sidewalk, Sundeep turned to walk back toward campus, but Oscar insisted that they go out for one more drink. He felt wanton and untethered. Sundeep tried to dissuade him, saw that he wouldn't be able to, and agreed. They headed back to the main strip, past the four undergrad bars where pitchers of beer cost nine dollars, and entered the grown-up bar where they cost twelve. Inside, Oscar walked directly to the bar, put down his credit card, and ordered two shots and two beers.

Here there was some haziness. The bar filled up and got louder and darker. He was talking with Sundeep one moment, and then in the next he was gone. Or had Oscar walked away from him? Was this a different bar? He discovered a fresh beer in his hands, which was wonderful.

Eventually, a woman emerged from the fog, leaning in over her drink to yell something into Oscar's ear. The music was loud and unfamiliar to him.

"What?" he yelled back, leaning closer.

"I said, I like your tweed jacket." They were both now angled in such a way, with his ear to her mouth, that he was looking straight down directly into her cleavage.

"Oh, this? They make us wear these."

"You teach at the school," she said.

"Yes," he said, not sure if it had been a question.

She laughed.

He took another sip of beer, which he found was actually

not beer but a glass of bourbon, and immediately lost the ability to track their conversation; he knew that he was talking although he couldn't quite make out the words. It felt like he was saying *mwah mwah mwah mwah*, but it didn't seem like that could actually be true. She touched his forearm. Whatever he was saying seemed to be agreeable.

His capability for thought was at this point reduced to the most broad and language-free concepts, and one of them was a general negativity or wrongness. There was something bad about this interaction, he knew that much, although he couldn't perceive it specifically at the moment. However, it did nothing to dull the appeal of sex. If anything, it added a certain desirable edge.

After another slip of time, she was leading him by the hand out the door, and soon they were coupled together in his bed, which rested on the floor without a frame. Of this scene he perceived little. He felt there was no verbal interaction at all, although there must have been. Just bodies, requesting and complying, a flash of pleasure, and the void of sleep.

When he awoke he was alone. His tongue was a pumice stone and he felt as if his brain pressed against his skull in all directions. He was able to fend off full consciousness for over an hour, as he sensed that there was something he would have to reckon with when he fully awoke. But it wasn't until he sat on the couch curled over a mug of coffee that he remembered that he had come home with anyone at all. He searched his phone but hadn't added any new numbers (there was however a series of texts from Sundeep trying to find him), and she hadn't left a note.

The only evidence that proved that she had even existed

at all was a hair clip that he found on the floor next to the bed, and a condom wrapper that fluttered down out of the sheets when he tore them up (which relieved him greatly). He couldn't remember what she looked like or what they had talked about.

"Yikes," he said out loud to himself, and then he thought that his lack of memory was probably for the best, as he put on his bathrobe and began to settle into a day of headaches and undifferentiated shame. This type of event was rare for Oscar, but not unheard of—depending on your definition, it was either his second or fourth one-night stand. He considered the issue closed.

Until that Monday in his intro class's third meeting of the semester, when he was passing out notes to accompany his lecture on Cartesian dualism, and dear God, there she was, sitting in the third row. While panic rose in his throat, he fought the urge to look in her direction until he thought that his refusal to move his head within a certain arc was becoming conspicuous, and then he allowed himself one glimpse at her, hoping at first that he might have been wrong and that it was really someone else, but she was still her, the memory of her face from that night suddenly clear now that he was presented with it.

She sat with her pen and notebook out, legs crossed, looking athletic, attractive, and, shit, younger than he remembered. He tried not to stare in horror. For the next hour, his mouth operated independently to deliver his remarks while in his mind he went through all the various ways he had ruined his life. What was the legal age of consent in this state, he wondered for the first time ever, his panic allowing some space for self-disgust. Encountering her now, after forgetting her, was like seeing a figure born out of a dream, a statue hewn in an unlit wing of his subconscious and then carted into view.

At the end of the lecture a few students stayed to ask him questions about the syllabus, and she lingered in the back of the pack. Oscar felt an odd mix of embarrassment and terror as he answered the other students' questions as quickly as he could. And then they were alone.

"Hi, Professor," she said. She held her books clutched across her chest. She had black hair that curled around her face like a set of parentheses, a small, mouse-like nose. She wore a loose-fitting rugby shirt, and her legs were clad in black yoga pants stuck into Red Wings.

"Hi, look…" he said, one hand on the back of his neck, the other jammed in a pocket, and came up with nothing. "Well, actually why don't you start off this interaction?"

"This is interesting territory," she said.

What a strange thing to say, Oscar thought.

"I'll be honest with you," Oscar said, "I don't remember anything."

"Nothing?"

"Not much."

"What does that change for me?"

"I guess I'd just like you to appreciate my confusion. My position."

"You have nothing to worry about."

"What happened—shouldn't have. It was…not proper. Given these circumstances, I mean, it appears."

"Oh please. I was completely sober, by the way. And whatever happens now can't retroactively alter the nature of the situation at the time, which seemed fine to me."

Oscar couldn't believe it.

"Did you know who I was?" he said.

"You mean, what your job is? Yeah, I knew, because you told me."

"So you must've not told me who you were."

"You mean that I was registered for your class? Yes, I told you that. You didn't seem to care."

Her eyes were dark brown, but as she spoke they took on a liveliness that Oscar couldn't place between malevolence or playfulness.

"Really?" Oscar said.

Oscar lowered his voice despite the fact that they were in a large, empty room and shot his eyes left and right in an almost comically conspiratorial gesture, despite himself. "Look— surely you understand how this has the potential to—reflect poorly on me."

She pulled her head back a little and regarded him. A look passed between them. "I've got to get to my next class. I'll see you Wednesday. Try not to freak out."

She turned and left. Oscar stood there stunned for a moment before ripping open his laptop to find her info in his class registration, which had headshot photos of all the students.

He said her name out loud when he found it, and in a flash that chamber of his memory was flooded with light, and he remembered her introducing herself to him at the bar.

"Dawn."

She was a junior. That meant that unless she had skipped a

grade, she was probably at least nineteen, maybe even twenty-one. So it appeared that he would not be going to jail. All that remained in jeopardy were his career, reputation, and self-respect.

With the shrugging horror of a man who had just narrowly avoided being hit by a bus, he realized that there was probably nothing to be done other than to pretend all of this had never happened. He resolved to never speak with her outside of class again.

Later that night, after grading papers, Oscar sat at his little desk hunched over his laptop under a pall of vengeful anger, eleven pages into a Google search trying to find more info on Paul St. Germaine, when there was a knock at his door.

Dawn stood right there on his doorstep.

"Hi! Can I come in?" She slipped past him before he could even register his shock. One of the St. Germaine videos was playing in a window on Oscar's laptop. On the screen, St. Germaine leaned back in his chair and said, "And why is it that you should be punished for the sins of the universe?"

"What're you watching?" Dawn said.

Oscar nearly leaped over the couch to clap closed the computer.

"Nothing," he said.

"Is that the guy you were telling me about?"

"God—I told you that? Wait a second, why are you here?"

Dawn sat down on his couch, looked around at his empty walls, dropped her bookbag at her feet. "Come on. Stop pretending you don't like me."

"I barely know you."

"You liked me enough to sleep with me."

"I was blackout drunk."

"Sure, but I could still tell."

"Dawn, I don't know what you think this is, but it was a huge mistake for me. I really think you should leave."

"Oh, screw you too, then." She did not seem actually upset. "And you finally remembered my name!"

"I could lose my job."

"Anyway—nobody knows."

"You don't know that! We were in public! Also, and I'm extremely uncomfortable with what I'm about to say, but... how old are you?"

"I'm twenty-two. Had a bit of a late start."

Guilty relief hit Oscar in a shudder of something like pleasure. He hadn't broken the law. He hadn't committed the crime that he allowed himself to finally consider the name of for the first time, now that he was innocent of it: statutory rape. "Holy shit, thank God," he said, momentarily covering his eyes with a hand.

He went and sat down on the opposite side of the couch.

"This is where you show me yours," she continued. "No way you're thirty..."

"I'm twenty-nine, actually."

"See! Totally within the realm."

"Dawn—you are my student."

"Well, yeah, I guess there is that."

"Which reminds me, I expect that you'll transfer out of my class."

Dawn laughed. She pulled a water bottle from the side pocket of her bookbag and took a sip. She drew her legs up under her on the couch. "No way. I find philosophy very interesting. And you're a great teacher."

"I'm okay."

"Yeah. You'll get better."

A silence.

"You know, I found your paper on JSTOR. Compatibilism. Fascinating stuff. Are we going to study that later in the semester?"

"In intro, only tangentially. We look a little deeper in my metaphysics class."

"It just seems a bit like cheating to me, to look at freedom and determinism and think, how about both?"

"Well, I know what you mean, but of course it's not that simple. For instance, as I mention in the paper, we can look at what Harry Frankfurt has written about the principle of alternate possibilities—" Oscar caught himself. "One second. I have yet to ascertain what you're doing here."

Dawn returned the water bottle to her bag. In one motion in which she placed her hand on the middle cushion and then dragged a knee along behind it, she crossed the couch and kissed him.

Oscar pulled his head back for one moment to say, "Ummm," and then she kissed him again and then he grabbed the sides of her head but not to move it away.

This type of situation was, he understood, totally unprecedented in his life, but he still thought that he would have mustered a little more willpower, or really any at all, to make what he knew to be the smart and moral choice. But he also understood, instantly and with full peace, that he wouldn't be able to reclaim control of this situation, and probably never had any in the first place.

They didn't speak. Memories returned to him of how it was the first time, the smell of her hair, the way she flipped her leggings off her foot while removing them. Everything else she left on. Soon she had unzipped his fly and he was inside her. They moved like that for a while, and then Oscar said, "Wait," and stood up and bent her over the arm of the couch.

After a minute like this, lost in a reddish energy that had moved in to surround him, he looked up and caught his reflection in the blackened window, and he didn't like the face that he saw.

"Here," he said and led her to his bedroom, moving quicker than his conscience. She took off the rest of her clothes and lay down while he swept laundry off the bed and took off his shirt and fumbled for a condom from his sock drawer.

"Hurry," she said. Then he was on top of her, entering again, and her fingernails dug into his back.

The entire time, Oscar thought, *Oh no, oh shit.*

Dawn said something quietly into his ear that he could not make out.

"Like this," she said, and took one of his hands and placed it softly around the front of her neck.

Oh no, oh shit, Oscar thought, as he tried squeezing, first only slightly and then a little more. She looked into his eyes, and what he saw there was cause for concern, but he pushed it away. He squeezed harder and heard a change in her breathing.

"Oh fuck," Dawn said. Oscar felt her start to climax. He shifted his weight and added his other hand to her neck and came powerfully.

He slumped to her side in a heap. She turned against his chest and continued to buck and spasm for a few moments, making sounds. He huffed for breath.

A minute later, after they had both quieted down, Oscar said, "Did I...did we...do that last time? The part at the end."

"We did," she said.

Rather than think, he fell deeply asleep almost immediately.

12

Just as the first time, when he woke up, she was gone. It was 2:00 a.m. He got out of bed and looked around. Again there was no evidence of her ever having been there. He still had no phone number for her. He sat down naked on his couch and opened his laptop to compose an email to Dawn's university address, which he pulled from his class list, and to which school authorities would have unfettered access, if they ever desired it in the future.

From<Oscar>
To<Dawn>
Subject: Office Hours
Hi Dawn,
Are you available to come to office hours tomorrow? There's something I'd like to discuss.
—OB

His cursor hovered over the send button for a moment and then, with the terrified bravery of a defeated general plunging his sword into his own abdomen, he clicked it. He wasn't sure why he did this but he told himself that he would figure it out later.

He found two beers in his fridge and drank them both quickly in an attempt to ease the constant dread that he had thought he would be more used to by this point, and got into bed and lay there and stared at the ceiling.

When he was a boy, he could lie awake in bed for an hour flexing a finger in front of his face and thinking, *Am I making this happen? What exactly is going on here?* He found it especially bewildering, in a wonderful way, that he could think the thought, "Move, finger," and the finger wouldn't move, but when he actually moved his finger, it required no such verbally imperative thought, and in fact seemed to happen with no type of thought at all on his part, or at least none that could be represented or described in another thought.

As he got older, though, his childish fascination metastasized into something else entirely, and now sometimes when he lay awake, the involutions of his own consciousness trying to perceive itself could drive him almost to tears. The thought of his own existence terrified him; not because he was afraid that it would one day cease to be, although that idea certainly wasn't cheery, but rather the inexplicability of it, the indescribable needlessness of it. He was embarrassed with the simplicity of the idea, and so never tried to give it the full weight of investigation that those in his field were supposed to be able to muster, and he never mentioned it to others, but it presented itself during these hours as the only question worth answering.

These thoughts would come only at night, and each time he would think, *How am I not obsessed with this all the time? How do people function?* But of course in the light of day, he would resume his routines immediately.

His night-thoughts and his day-thoughts were more than just entirely different sets of thoughts; they were entirely different modes of being. Even when during the day he paused to suss out a point in a paper he was reading or to spar with an astute student (in other words, when he was "doing philosophy"), his thoughts had a way of functioning alongside language: solving problems, achieving tasks, figuring things out through dialectic. But in the dark, his thoughts became unhinged from physical or linguistic application and floated above him as a meaningless terror.

At 4:00 a.m., he rose from bed to check his email to see if Dawn had responded. She hadn't. He urinated and then drank another beer standing up in his kitchen, to combat the dry mouth. He lay in bed and masturbated as a purely utilitarian gesture, trying to coax some more dopamine out of his brain in order to get to sleep.

When he awoke again, the first thing he felt was surprise that he had actually fallen asleep. Still in bed, he checked his email.

From<Dawn>
To<Oscar>
Subject: Office Hours
2?

A number and a question mark. Not much to analyze. Trying to be cool, to combat her flippancy with some of his own, he wrote back, Sure, and sent it, and then immediately regretted it. It would be obvious to her that he was trying to armor himself, trying to compete, although he had no leverage at all. He may as well go to her on his knees.

The morning was a waste. He thought he might be able to escape into the paper he had been trying to develop, which was a further explication of his first one on compatibilism, but he found it impossible to focus and soon gave up. He paced back and forth in his kitchen trying to summon the bravery to examine the university handbook to see if relations with students were expressly forbidden or just highly frowned upon, but could not. He considered calling his father to check in, but could not. He rode his bike onto campus, taught his one class, and then went to his office to wait for her.

Oscar's "office" was the size of a rich person's closet. The room was a simple rectangle barely twice the size of his desk, which bisected the space, and there was one small window that looked out onto a small courtyard. The effect was claustrophobic rather than nookish, which was not conducive to a vibrant mental landscape, and Oscar used it only to hold his mandatory office hours twice each week. He kept a few books on the shelves: one of his three copies of *The Republic* festooned with sticky notes, Aristotle, Kant, Hume, and Schopenhauer, a personal favorite.

At exactly 2:00 p.m., Dawn walked in and shut the door behind her, although it had been open. She sat down on the other side of the desk in one of the two Windsor-back chairs, thunking her bookbag into the other.

"Hi, Professor," she said. She wore jeans and a wrinkled white blouse.

"Hello," he said. "Could you just——?" He held up one finger. He stood and went to the door and opened it again, and then returned to his seat.

Dawn made a tiny sound through her nose that was something like one-tenth of a laugh.

"This is your office?" she said. There was a note of familiarity in her tone that Oscar thought was unearned.

"I don't like it either."

"It's not that bad. Get some art up maybe. A nice lamp."

"I really only meet students here. I do most of my work in the library."

"Ah," she said, raising her eyebrows and looking around, waiting for whatever was about to happen.

"Obviously this is weird. I'm sorry about that," Oscar said. "But I'll be direct and admit that this is coming from a position of pure self-interest, as I like my job, and I don't want to lose it. Did you tell anyone about what happened with us?"

He used the word "happened" to try to contain it in the past. A single incident.

Dawn smiled and looked down slightly, seeming either amused or annoyed. "I mean, look, this is college. Things get said, people talk. Everyone's drunk all the time. It's hard to keep track of who knows what."

Oscar received this with pursed lips. He went back over to the door and closed it softly, and then returned to his desk and looked Dawn directly in her eyes. He recalled that her eyes were brown, but in this lighting they appeared to be nearly black.

"Yeah, Dawn, listen. Here's where I'm at. My mother just died a terrible, undignified death. I loved her very much but never expressed it well. She and my father were on the way back from giving away all of their money to a cult leader who had promised to cure her depression, which I may or may not have inherited; I mean inherited the depression, not the money, which is gone. My father is now relying on me to help him find meaning in his life again, or just support him financially, I'm not sure, because his relationship with my sister is even worse than his relationship with me, which is terrible. I made twenty-two thousand dollars last year before taxes, I'm very lonely, lately it's become clear to me that life is a period of meaninglessness broken up by moments of pain and bookended by nothingness, and I think my career may be in jeopardy here, so I'd like for you to please tell me honestly, because I need to know—did you tell anyone about what happened between us?"

"You know, you told me all of that already. Also your sister is getting divorced."

"Please answer the question."

Dawn took a second to think.

"Okay, you see here, now I'm getting a little bit mad, because it's a bullshit question. You want to know if I ran home shouting, 'Hey, hey, I just fucked a professor'? Or do you want to know if there's a chance that one of the several friends that I was at that bar with, because of course I was there with friends, saw me leave with you? To the former I say screw you, and to the latter I say how the hell should I know?"

She didn't yell or even get animated while she spoke, but her face took on a pointed fury that Oscar recognized as a kind of pugilism. She was enjoying this, in a certain way.

"And you know what, fine," she said. "I thought maybe I liked you but this is me officially requesting that you leave me alone. Congratulations. Christ."

Dawn got up and moved to the door and opened it. She stood in the doorway and turned back to him. She looked at the floor briefly and then back up at him. Her face had regained its normal rounded edges. She took a breath.

"I'm sorry I got mad. I actually think you're a sweet guy. And I'm sorry your mom died. That's terrible. Still though, fuck you."

Oscar stared at a point on his desktop, wondering where to go from here. He crossed his arms over his chest and exhaled. Her eyes lingered on him for a moment and then she turned to go.

"Wait," Oscar said.

She turned back.

"Listen, I didn't mean—"

"I know," Dawn said. "You're a mess, but you'll get some of this stuff figured out."

And with that she left.

When Oscar got back home, there were two emails from Dawn in his inbox, sent five minutes apart:

Professor,
I realize now that I wouldn't have said what I said in your office if I didn't at least subconsciously consider myself as occupying some sort of privileged position re: you. For instance

I couldn't imagine saying the F-word in front of a prof under normal circumstances, or referring to them as "a sweet guy." So I apologize for that.

Also I guess I was being a little disingenuous or evasive when I said that I didn't know who knew about what happened with us. The truth is this: my friends saw me leave with you. Later they tried to find out what happened but I didn't tell them anything, because I'm like that, contrary to what you might think.

Best,

D

The second email read:

I regret sending that last email. Let's just please forget about it.

Oscar counted this as some kind of minor victory, for her to share at least a little in his discomfort.

As he sat there looking at his inbox, a new email popped in the top of the queue from the assistant to the chair of the philosophy department, with the subject line YOUR IMMEDI-ATE RESPONSE REQUESTED. Blood rushed to his face. With icy terror, already halfway prepared to accept his ignomini-ous firing, he clicked on it, and there was so much text in the window that opened that he panicked and clicked out. He told himself that he would read this later, when he was in a bet-ter mental state. For the moment, he preferred to not know.

Under normal circumstances, these emails would have preoccupied him entirely. But for the rest of the day, he found that he could not stop thinking about St. Germaine.

He felt robbed in a deeply personal way that gnawed at him constantly. The fact was that there was a man out there somewhere who had taken his family's money, money that was made by his parents' honest and underpaid work, work that had overpaid for Oscar to pursue an interest that was, even for the Academy, the hardest to justify economically. But it wasn't just the money; there was also something further, something about his mother's death that he could not convince himself was coincidental. For her to have just *died*—he was, it turned out, unable to accept it. There must have been more to it. St. Germaine would have answers. He had to.

Oscar couldn't name the resolution that he desired, exactly. He wasn't feeling violent, although he was certainly filled with anger, and he had actually never been prone to acts of violence and so wouldn't have been able to accurately say what the prelude to a violent act felt like. He just thought it might be good to know at least where the guy even was.

He pored over the search engine results again, the same low-activity message boards, the same outdated pictures. He even signed up for an account with one forum just so that he could leave a query asking if anyone knew how to contact St. Germaine. He found a phone number listed on St. Germaine's website, but when he called it, it was out of service. There was no email or physical address listed.

Sitting there at his little table, Oscar's hatred began to build. This guy, this fucking guy, who considered himself some kind of philosopher, thought he knew what was good for Oscar's mother. He thought he was a philosopher because he tricked sad, vulnerable people into thinking he was smart? I *am a fucking philosopher,* Oscar thought. I *know what it means to actually try to use nothing but thought to move closer to a description of reality.* I *am doing the real work of perception.*

As he pulled the cap from a bottle of cheap bourbon that he had bought on the way home, he thought about how you go through your life hoping that you'll sneak past the hounds of catastrophe without letting them get your scent, you hope you don't get horribly burned, don't drink two beers and then drive and obliterate a family in a wreck, don't have a child and love it and then be forced to watch it die of some ingeniously horrific disease, don't get framed for murder and rot innocent in jail. But sometimes people's lives just up and go to shit. He could feel it beginning to happen now, his life listing into the tilt that would precede a topple.

Could the solution be something as simple as money? No, certainly not.

But it was a start.

He opened his laptop, and then a blank email.

Mr. St. Germaine, he began.

My name is Oscar Boatwright. You may remember my mother, Delia, who was a big fan of yours, I'm told, and who I believe met with you several times. I'm sorry to have tell you this, if in fact you do remember her, but she has unfortunately passed away quite suddenly. As you might expect, we are all quite broken up over losing her.

Like you, I am interested in the mind, and in free will in particular. I am in fact an assistant professor of philosophy, with a focus on metaphysics. I've been watching some of your seminars, and although I'm not finished yet, I have some questions. For one—do you have any degrees? I'll be honest: I'm not sure that your premises support your conclusions. But what I'm more interested in is obtaining a better idea of what was going on in my mother's head in what proved to be her last days—as I understand it, your methods were of great comfort to her. Can you tell me any of what the two of you discussed? What she said? Anything really.

I'd love it if you'd respond. You can call me at the below phone number at any time, or if you're located somewhere on the west coast, I'd be happy to come find you.

Please, I do hope you get back to me.

Sincerely,

Oscar Boatwright

P.S. Can I have my inheritance back, motherfucker?

Oscar leaned back, took another swig of bourbon, and reread what he had written. After a moment of catharsis, he highlighted the text and prepared to delete it, but then he had an idea. He opened a blank spreadsheet and started listing possible email addresses: PSG, PSGermaine, Paul.St.Germaine. After a few minutes he had several dozen guesses. He then duplicated each one with an @ sign and the five biggest email providers he could think of offhand.

Acting quickly, before he could stop himself, he copied this list of hundreds of email addresses into the bcc line of the email he had composed, added the subject line For Paul St. Germaine, and, after a moment's circumspection, deleted the postscript. With one more drink, he hit Send and regretted it instantly, somehow in fact even one instant before his finger had clicked the button. He closed his laptop as the undeliverable notices began to flood his inbox, and went to bed, hating himself.

The next day, as he was standing in his kitchen making coffee, trying to focus on small things one at a time, his cell phone rang. Number unknown.

"Hi, Oscar?" she said when he answered. "I mean, Professor? I got your phone number from the campus directory. I've got something I'd like to talk about. Could you meet me somewhere? This is Dawn, by the way."

"Can it not wait for office hours? What's going on?"

"I shouldn't say over the phone."

13

One thing, at least, was perfectly clear: he should not be doing this. He should not be going to an off-campus address to meet with a student he had slept with and whose motives were still unknown to him, especially given that she had sounded additionally out of sorts on the phone when she told him that it couldn't wait until tomorrow.

This he had taken as something of a threat. He decided that he would go, partly due to the worry that she could still easily ruin him if he were to make her unhappy and partly due to an embarrassingly earnest and inextinguishable impulse to aid someone who needed help. As he grabbed his bike helmet, he realized that there was a third reason: he might be trying to hide from himself an actual fondness for her. This was a terrifying notion.

The address was for a unit within a condo complex that, according to the sign at the front gate, was called Evergreen Estates. He had never seen it before. There were no evergreen trees in sight, and in fact the grounds seemed almost completely defoliated, in the manner of all hastily constructed suburban housing developments. The design was wooden faux-rustic but clearly very new, and the parking lot, which ringed the central hub of buildings, was only about 10 percent full.

He consulted with the house number that he had scrawled on a shred of paper and found the right unit, in the heel of the U-shaped building layout. He locked his bike to a lamppost out front and walked up the steps above the garage door.

The door was open but he knocked anyway.

"He's here," he heard a male voice say from within.

Dawn came to the door wearing a university sweatshirt and pajama bottoms, her hair in a bun. "Professor! Come in."

The main room, which was connected to the kitchen, was appointed in an artlessly affluent style that indicated that the place had come pre-furnished by the real estate company. A black leather couch and loveseat formed an L around a glass and brushed-steel coffee table. On the wall were several framed prints of desert and alpine landscapes and an enormous plasma screen TV played sports highlights on mute. An ionizing fan swiveled its dumb head in the corner. On the loveseat sat a young man in jeans and a white T-shirt.

"Please, sit," Dawn said, gesturing toward the couch. "Can I get you some water?" She went to the sink.

Oscar sat.

"Nice bike," said the man.

"Thanks," said Oscar, feeling more lost by the second.

"Professor, this is Ramos," Dawn called from the kitchen. "Ramos, Professor Boatwright."

"Hi, Professor," Ramos said, not offering his hand. He looked to be about twenty-one, with a lean, angular face and jet-black hair down to his neck. His muscles were knobby under his T-shirt. He picked his nails with a folding blade not quite long enough to be overtly sinister, but almost. Oscar managed a smile in his direction.

Dawn brought a glass of water clinking with ice and set it down in front of Oscar and sat at the other end of the couch between him and Ramos. She curled her bare feet under her thighs on the couch.

"Ramos is the campus drug dealer. Well, one of them."

Oscar spit some of the water he was drinking back into the cup.

"That's me," Ramos said.

Oscar forced a nervous laugh.

"Yeah, only I'm not kidding though," said Dawn. "But it's cool."

"We know you're cool," said Ramos, folding the knife and returning it to his pocket.

Oscar had an animal instinct to bolt for the door, but his legs felt momentarily powerless. "I see," he said, mind whirring.

"Right, sorry. So? Should we just get right into it?" She looked at Ramos and made a *why not?* face. "I had an idea," she said. "Something we could do together. This is something that I think could help you big-time. But let me say first—I know you'll keep an open mind."

"Okay," Oscar said, shifting in his seat.

"It's not that hard of a thing," said Ramos.

"Really kind of absurdly easy, actually," she said. "All you'd need to do is drive somewhere, pick something up, and drive back."

Oscar felt himself dissociate from the scene only slightly, so that everything pulsated with absurdity. Things had moved from confusing to scary to hilarious all in just a few seconds. He couldn't think of anything to say. What the fuck was going on here? Who were these fucking kids?

"I don't have a car," he said.

Dawn and Ramos looked at each other.

"That's your first concern?" she said. "We'll get that figured out. We'll get you a car."

"How many gears on your bike?" Ramos said.

Oscar ignored him. He felt sweat form on his forehead, blood rush to his face, his vision of the future swing out wildly over a yawning gulf, his stomach cold and leaden.

"So this is like, I take it, a pretty much illegal thing you're asking me to do," Oscar said.

Dawn and Ramos shared a look.

"Let's just stick to the when/where details for a minute," Dawn said.

Ramos was playing with the knife again. "You'd just be going for a drive, my guy. Nothing so tricky about that."

Oscar felt real fear now. He could guess the rest of this but some part of him would hold out against the truth until he heard it spoken.

Dawn continued, "I've been thinking about your financial situation. Your parents, your sister, student loans. I know they pay you shit here. And now an opportunity has come up, and I arrived at the conclusion that if there was thirty thousand dollars to be made in a weekend that you might be in the exactly correct position to be interested in it."

Oscar hunched over. The entrance of money into this conversation had caught him off guard and he could not hide his immediate desire. "Holy crap," he said.

"I know," Dawn said. "Big number!"

"And this is the kind of thing that you've…done before?"

"Good question. Not exactly. But I will tell you, I do this because I'm smart and good at it and I don't raise suspicions and this school is expensive."

"Fuck a student loan," Ramos said.

Dawn continued, "And I don't want to go into specifics, but although Ramos and I are familiar with this industry, we haven't yet required a drive of this distance, and I don't have a driver's license and Ramos is a brown man."

"It's fucked up but it's true," Ramos said. "I get stopped on my way to pick up my kid from school."

"And what's going on here, exactly?" Oscar said, gesturing between her and Ramos.

"I don't think you need to know the exact structure of our relationship. Partners. Let's focus on the proposition at hand."

Oscar blinked and looked back and forth between them. He remained silent as he felt the inescapable gravity of very large things draw him closer against his will. Ramos lit a cigarette.

"I know," Dawn said. "This is weird. You're learning all kinds of things about who I actually am versus who I appear to be. Which is a little shocking. But there's really nothing so crazy going on. Currently, until I save up enough to cover my student debt and maybe grad school, I am what must be called 'a drug dealer.' Plenty of people are—I don't run from the term. And like most things that I do, I'm good at it."

"You know, I really wouldn't have guessed," Oscar said.

"That's the idea."

Some of Oscar's critical faculties began to come back on-line. He sat up and brought his pursed fingers to his lips. He took a moment to laugh at himself for ever thinking that this person might have counted sleeping with her professor as an illicit thrill.

"Okay, so," he said, "how are you so comfortable telling me all this? How do you know I won't...tell someone?" As he asked, Oscar already knew the answer and that he would surely never breathe a word of this to anyone.

"Well, for one, you like me, and I know you wouldn't want to ruin my life. But also, I think you know the answer to your own question. Please don't make me say it. I'm honestly bringing this to you in your best interest. Do you know how many people would jump at this opportunity? I could be on the phone and find somebody in an hour, probably."

"Blackmail," Oscar said, mostly just to see how it would feel when describing the actual state of affairs.

"That's the word I didn't want to say, but, yes, sure, fine, you won't go to the school or to the police because I never told anybody about what happened between us, but I could, and I could even elaborate. God, now I feel like such a dick. And anyway, I'm completely insulated from anything incriminating in ways that I won't explain to you for obvious reasons. Suffice it to say that my hands, hard drives, et cetera are all squeaky clean. And the school doesn't even know Ramos exists."

"Ramos isn't even my real name," Ramos said. "Ramos is just some motherfucker I heard about once."

Ramos leaned forward on his knees and looked at Oscar intently for the first time. He seemed to come alive in an instant, rush forward toward the brink of something. "And please look me in the eyes so I can tell you that I'm an underprivileged young man with a kid to feed, I've got all kinds of issues going on, and if you fuck this shit up for me, I will fucking hurt a dude."

Oscar tried to appear unaffected as his nervous system fired in alarm.

"Ramos!" Dawn said. "Come on. None of that. That's not cool. We talked about this." Dawn turned to Oscar. "I'm sorry. He apologizes. That's totally not in keeping with the spirit of partnership that I expect us to close on here."

Dawn shot a sustained look at Ramos until he sat back again in his seat.

"I apologize," Ramos said.

Now that the threat of physical harm was out on the table, things seemed oddly defused, rather than escalated.

"You know," Oscar said, "the school might already know about us. I got an email from my department chair. I didn't read the whole thing."

"Well, I don't know what to tell you about that. Wasn't me."

Oscar looked at Ramos, who was lighting up another cigarette. "They let you smoke in rentals like this?"

"Haven't checked."

Oscar found himself laughing. It turned out that total abandon had a very distinct edge of comedy to it. "You haven't even explained what it is you want me to do."

Dawn smiled. "Finally you ask."

She reached under the coffee table and produced a map that had been printed from the internet.

"Couldn't be simpler," she said, handing it over. "Here's where you'd be going. You can do it in ten hours each way if you don't hit traffic."

Oscar looked at the map. The red destination pin jutted out of somewhere south of San Diego.

"Mexico," Oscar said.

"No. Just close. It's kind of in the middle of nowhere but a GPS will get you there no problem. There, you'll be given a package."

"What kind of package?"

"Nothing crazy. Backpack-sized."

"I mean, what of?"

"Oscar." She looked at him as if he was a child. "Illegal drugs."

Oscar tried to keep his face from twitching. Throughout everything that he had been going through, he had remained more or less confident in his vision of himself as manfully stoic and resolute. But this threatened to break him.

"I don't want to say the words 'why me,'" Oscar said, "but—I can't do this. I could never do this. You must know that. This is like, a joke. Why would you even bring this to me?"

Dawn's face reversed polarity yet again. Any malice that he thought he might have detected was gone.

"It will be more clear to you when I hand you a fat manila envelope stuffed full of hundred dollar bills. You're in trouble, Oscar, but I know what you need. You should consider me your angel."

Oscar felt that much of what he had thought he had known about the world and his life had been finally cut away from him after a period of sawing that started with his mother's death and that now he was drifting away on a small chunk of it toward something else. One set of truths receded and a new one came into focus.

He dropped his head into his palm and kneaded it, laughed, and then moaned. "Come on. I mean, Jesus. Can't you see I'm coming apart here? And this is what you do to me?"

Dawn put her hand on Oscar's back, rubbed it.

"Everything's going to be okay, Oscar. But we need to move soon. Give it some thought."

14

While biking home, Oscar assessed the situation. In his head, he heard the voice of St. Germaine telling him that it was already determined. But even if the invisible future already existed immutably, he ran through different scenarios in his head, trying to find points where he might salvage even a semblance of control.

Like it or not, he told himself, he was in this thing now, and the only way out, went something he had heard once, was through. It felt good to hug this thought for an instant, but then he realized that it didn't really mean anything.

Of course, it went without saying that he would never be capable of doing something like this. He had essentially never committed a crime in his life. Once in his youth, he had shoplifted some baseball cards from a local drugstore out of some urge to prove that he was cool, but of his own volition he returned the next day in tears to confess his sin to the proprietor and offer him a handful of sweaty quarters.

The very idea of breaking the law was abhorrent to him, cut against everything he believed about society and civilization and how one should act within it. To say nothing of his respect for (or if you'd prefer, fear of) authority, which was equally immense. He had never even been ticketed for a moving violation.

And even setting moral considerations aside! He would, on a purely practical level, be terrible for what she was asking. His nerves were jangly. His stomach rebelled under stress. He was not great at improvisation. He scrounged for more reasons: he…was very busy with schoolwork.

Eventually his thoughts returned to the money.

Oscar had always envied those who seemed to understand something about where money could be found, the direction of will that was required to generate it. It was something that Oscar had long ago decided he would never be able to grasp, and so had done his best to prune his desire for money completely. Although he knew that there were other ways to make money (there simply had to be!), he wasn't able to name any just right at this moment.

Thirty thousand dollars.

He hated thinking about money. He had never had more than $2,800 in his accounts at any one point of his life. That was after his college graduation, when several gift checks hit at once. But then of course he had jumped immediately into grad school and made the acquaintance of his new life companion, $73,000 dollars of debt, of which he had so far been able to pay back $2,000.

He wondered if the story of his life was going to be the

story only of an intelligent coward who used a vague moral superiority to mask his inaction.

His *life*, that word—there were plenty of them out there just like it. *What makes mine so special that I'm not allowed to maybe ruin it?*

He stopped pedaling his bike and coasted to a stop; put his feet on the ground.

Honestly, fuck it. Fuck it! I'll go. Wait—that's absurd. I can't go.

The very thought chilled him in a shiver. He knew nothing about any of this.

Drugs? I'm a drug dealer now? Not even a dealer. A mule. For a pretty little kingpin.

He had to be smart about this.

The real truth of it, the scariest one, the one that he felt was slowly sapping his defenses, was that, although this was ridiculous, in a dark, agitating, physical way, the idea excited him.

For the second time, he resolved never to speak to Dawn again. This time for real.

15

When he walked into his apartment that night, he sat at his table and called his father immediately. Lee picked up after four rings.

"Hey, Oscar. Little late here. Everything okay?"

"Sorry about the time. I was just—thinking about you. How are you doing?"

"Fine. Your sister was over earlier. Your voice sounds funny. Is something wrong?"

Oscar held a balled fist up against his brow. "I was calling to see how *you* were doing."

"Nothing has changed, I suppose."

"Yeah. Yeah. Well. I guess that's not really what I mean."

"Oscar, thank you, but I don't need checking up on."

"Dad, please—you can stop being like this."

There was silence on the line. Oscar wondered at which of the two phones in the house Lee was speaking—either the one in the kitchen or the one on his mother's nightstand. Oscar heard Lee sigh deeply.

"Okay. I'll tell you. The hardest part," Lee said, and stopped. "The hardest part is waking up. There's an instant every morning where I forget that she's gone. And then I turn to look at her or reach out for her, and there's nothing, just a cold empty space in the bed, and each day it's all I can do to keep from screaming out right there. It's awful—it's just so awful. I keep thinking, how can this be part of life and still so awful? How have so many people gone through this? How can this be real?"

"Yes. It's very strange," Oscar said. "But I do feel like she's with me in some way. Watching over my shoulder, or from above, maybe." Oscar didn't feel this at all, but it seemed like a good thing to say.

Lee laughed bitterly. "I don't. Let's not become childish. I don't feel anything. Anything good, I mean."

Oscar slumped down out of his chair and lay down flat on the kitchen floor. The tiles were cold on his back. He draped the arm not holding the phone over his eyes to shield them from the overhead light.

"Okay, Dad. Thanks for telling me that."

"Well. I think I'll be going to bed now. I'm glad you called."

"Good night, Dad."

Oscar stood back up, found his laptop, found the half-full bottle of bourbon, took a double swig like a man about to have his leg amputated in a tent, and started one of the videos up at a random point in the middle as he fought down the burn.

You total bastard, Oscar thought when he saw St. Germaine leaning forward in his little chair with his little plant.

"Ask yourself," he was saying, "when did you decide to be the person you are? What steps did you take to construct your world around you? Or did you not build it at all? What if it was forced on you? What if you were actually imprisoned there, imprisoned in yourself? If I gave you a match, would you burn your prison down?"

Oscar drank and watched more videos until the bottle was empty, slipped through time, and woke up on the floor at 5:00 a.m. While still on the floor, held there as if under a net of anxiety and disgust, he looked at his phone, and found that he had texted Dawn at two in the morning:

Can we meet?

and she had responded two minutes later:

No texting.

He stood up, took one step, and then lurched for the sink and vomited brown acid into the drain. He wiped his mouth, stumbled to the couch, and deleted the texts before passing back out.

His preprogrammed alarm woke him up in time to shower and he made it to his intro class fifteen minutes late. While he struggled through his lecture on Spinoza's determinism, he thought he could sense his students looking at him differently, as if something was off. He could not look at Dawn, who sat in the front row and spoke up several times during discussion at length; perhaps, he felt, to bail him out. After he ended the class (ten minutes early), she waited while the other students filed out, and then came up to him.

"Late night?" she said.

Oscar said nothing.

"I should have told you that I don't really like to text."

"Yeah, sure, that makes sense," he said.

She tilted her head. "So, did you want me to come over?"

"I don't know what I wanted."

"I think you did."

Oscar laughed. "Please spare a thought for my internal state. I'm not even one hundred percent sure that I'm awake right now."

"You're awake, I promise. Look at the clock—that's one way to tell. In dreams, numbers on the dial are all messed up, smushed to one side or shifting around."

There was a clock on the wall by the door and they looked at it together.

"I think I probably wanted some further discussion about the...matter at hand."

"Okay, look, how about this, I have another class I need to get to now, but can you meet me tonight? Off campus."

She suggested that they meet somewhere she thought he wouldn't be worried about being seen together—the bar of a blue-collar bowling alley a dozen miles from campus. He borrowed Sundeep's car. She was waiting for him on a barstool when he got there.

They ordered Coors Lights that came in frosted glasses and a basket of fries to split.

"Okay, look," Dawn said, over the clatter of flying pins and '80s rock. "I know you think that this is like the biggest deal in the world, to do something like this, to dip a toe in this world. I thought so, too, at the start. But I want you to realize just how common this is, just how many people are doing it. Every time you see something on the news, with cops lining up bricks on the curb outside a box truck? That is like a lightning strike, compared to everything that gets through. No, not like a lightning strike, because lightning is random—this is even less likely because you can change your odds by being smart. Those people on the news were stupid—I can point out a big mistake in almost every case. You are smart. I am smart. We have everything worked out. I promise you that this will be fine."

"The money is—it's incredible."

"Yes, it is. And I hope you trust that I've been honest with you and that I will give you all that you've been promised."

"I do, actually. Ha, how stupid is that." Oscar took a long drink from his glass.

"I am happy with the profit that I'll be clearing. I have no reservations about giving you what you are owed for this. This is not a rare thing, like I said, but we do need you. Your white maleness is extremely valuable. It will protect you as it always has. I bet you've never been pulled over on the highway once in your life."

She was right.

"You won't have problems recouping that cash when I get—if I got it here?"

"No."

"How—?"

"Listen, Oscar, for reasons that I'm sure will make sense to you, I want to keep you sequestered from the big picture here as much as possible, okay? Also, that reminds me, I want you to promise—no Google."

"What?"

"You know how when you have a weird pain that you can't explain so you get on the internet and the next thing you know you've convinced yourself that you have several types of cancer and have begun to consider your own funeral arrangements? That applies here—don't Google the law, don't Google how other people have done it, don't even Google the route. It can only hurt you. It will drain your nerve and nerve is the only thing you need for this. I know it's asking a lot but I think it would be best if you trusted me."

Behind them, someone bowled a strike and bellowed, "Hell yeah!"

"When would I have to go?"

"Tomorrow morning."

His heart rate spiked. "And what if I didn't?"

"Wheels are in motion. We are now counting on you. This is a one-time offer. If you bail, which you won't because you can't, but if you did I'd have to scramble to find someone else."

Oscar finished his beer.

"I need you to decide right now," Dawn said. "Don't think. Decide."

Oscar thought of his father, suffering alone in his house, heat turned down as low as possible to save money, sorting through the basement for anything that could be sold. He thought of the .308 propped up in the corner of his father's broom closet. He thought of his sister, his imagination taking over now, crying silently over the bed of her youngest son. He thought of his mother, hurting so bad that she saw fit to hand over her last dollar to a stranger, or worse yet, she knew it was wrong but would do anything to make the pain stop. All of this horror seemed like it was about 40 percent related to money. And how much of it could thirty thousand even alleviate?

He saw his father's broken face, the way he looked at the grave of his wife. He saw his sister holding her son's hand, weeping for more than he realized. He saw his student loan statement. Suddenly his heart was filled with an inexplicable, terrible longing.

"Okay," Oscar said, and exhaled. "Okay okay okay okay okay."

PART II

16

Oscar woke early. He had thought that he might not have been able to sleep, but he had one of the most restful nights of his life, with entirely untranslatable dreams about red and yellow spheres of light dancing around columns of rock in an underwater cave. The memory of these dreams immediately began to slip away from him, like running ink.

Outside the sky was a very dark blue. His body pulsed in rolling waves that he felt down to his fingertips. He dressed in his favorite clothes, to fortify his spirit: jeans nearly worn out in the thighs but still strong at the seams, Piggly Wiggly T-shirt, brown leather jacket starting to crack at the elbows. He pulled on his boots like armored greaves. He was too nervous to eat but he took his time brewing coffee and sat in a kitchen chair by the window watching the sun slowly suggest itself.

He checked his email one more time, since he wouldn't be able to check it from his flip phone. At the top of the screen sat an email from PSGermaine@yahoo.com. His blood paused in his veins.

His cursor moved to click it but then he remembered what Dawn had said about maintaining his will. *Now is not the time,* he told himself. But he jammed the laptop into his backpack so he could read it later, along with the email from the philosophy department. Out the front window, he saw that the car was parked on the street just like Dawn said it would be; a recent-model silver Range Rover with sport trim and a large, aggressive-looking deer guard set out in front of the grill. He imagined the almost tender image of her and Ramos coming by to drop it off in the middle of the night, wordless, communicating with flicks of the eyes. The keys were waiting for him in his mailbox.

He walked one lap around the car, opened the door and jumped in. New car smell engulfed him.

On the gleaming wood-panel dash was a yellow Post-it:

The GPS is already programmed. XOXO

Oscar pulled off the note and crumpled it up. He remembered a joke he had heard once: How do you fuck an elephant? You just climb on up there and start fucking.

He put the key in the ignition and the car came to life in two stages, implying a turbocharger. He felt the engine thrum powerfully, beg to get moving. If he was going to do this, which it appeared that he was, he'd better not do it halfway. "You're fine," he said out loud to himself. "It's cool. This is cool." He put on his black sunglasses, even though it was still barely light outside, and looked at himself in the rearview mirror. He was almost convinced.

He tried to converse with his interior monologue but found it to be basically an unending scream.

The soothing voice of the British woman in the GPS got him onto the highway headed south. The sun was up now, reflecting low off the hood and warming Oscar's arms and chest. He realized that his current level of nervousness would fry him out if he were to drive like this for ten hours, so he took deep breaths and tried to let his mind wander. He fiddled with the radio, found NPR, and returned his hands to the wheel. He listened to three minutes of a piece about people who had been forced to sell their homes and live in converted vans before he caught himself and quickly flipped to a rock station: T. Rex. He rolled down the windows and draped his left arm over the door panel. It was hot out and getting hotter. He turned up the music.

The car was a beast. It was hard to believe that something so large could be so quick, but he zipped around trucks with ease and caught himself creeping over eighty more than once, which startled him. The last thing he needed right now was to be pulled over, although he supposed it would be an even bigger issue on the way back. He set the cruise control to three miles per hour below the speed limit.

In this way, he passed the first hour, burning off the adrenaline. It took about that long for him to realize that if something terrible was going to happen, it probably wouldn't happen today, so he might as well relax.

Oscar couldn't remember the last time he had taken a long car trip. It had been so easy to remain cloistered at the university that he had never seen any reason to deal with the hassles and costs of owning a car, even in California, but now he began to think twice about that decision. He had forgotten how meditative the act of driving could be, under the right conditions. He thought that it probably had something to do with the fact that such an easy and simple-seeming action (find a lane, maintain a speed, stay within the lines) was so effective at hiding a truth that should have been obvious: that he was in direct control of an enormous hunk of metal that could end his life and the lives of others with a simple jerk of the wheel.

Around eleven o'clock his lack of breakfast caught up with him and he pulled into a truck stop. He bought black coffee and two tamales from under a heat lamp, paid the Mexican girl behind the counter who couldn't have been more than thirteen years old, and sat in a booth facing the parking lot to eat. Before he left, he went back to the counter and paid for a pack of Marlboros and a lighter. He had smoked maybe ten cigarettes in his life and had never enjoyed them, but they might make a good prop for the character he was playing.

Back on the road he lit one up and decided that he was right. He coughed at first but found that the nicotine both steadied and enlivened him. He laughed when he thought of Dawn being annoyed that he had smoked inside her car. Was this even her car?

"Screw you, anyway," he said out loud, and smiled.

The sun rose to its peak and then began to fall and still Oscar was going south, the red line on the GPS that separated him from his destination steadily shortening. The palette of the scenery outside his window changed from greens to brown, vegetation to sand and sagebrush.

There was not a single instant that he didn't feel a burning, physically uncomfortable urge to turn around immediately. It was only to his own amazement that he had, as of yet, not.

When the GPS indicated that he was two hours from the location where it was supposed to happen, he began to come out of his trance. Soon he would again have to exit the car and make the minor decisions that constituted moving through the world.

He began to keep his eyes open for a motel when he was sixty miles out from the point. He passed up a Motel 6 in favor of some place called the Circled Wagons Inn. The parking lot was one-quarter filled with trailer-less trucks and dusty SUVs. He parked, went into the office, and paid the smoking woman at the desk twenty-six dollars cash for the night.

Oscar brought his bag into the room, which was on the second level facing the empty pool, and sat on the bed. *Not so bad*, he thought.

On the other side of the road he could see a chain steakhouse with the outline of the state of Texas and the words Open Late! in neon. He locked his door, walked across the parking lot, darted across the road through traffic, and entered.

There were only a handful of customers inside, and when the hostess led him to a table, he asked if he could have the big corner booth, which he had always preferred since childhood— something about having a solid wall behind him.

"Well, hey, it's fine with me," she said. "Haven't had a party of eight in forever."

He sat alone at the booth under a wall covered with cattle skulls and wagon wheels and fake Indian war clubs. When the waitress came (were there any males in this town?) he ordered the largest steak they had, adding, "I know you guys aren't allowed to serve it very rare, but what if I said pretty please?"

She smiled and said she'd see if she could pull some strings.

As he waited for his steak, he drank two beers and listened to the piped-in mariachi music. The slab of meat came out flanked by a baked potato and crispy onions. It swam in its own blood. He ate every bite.

Back in his room, Oscar got his laptop out of his bag to finally read the email that had been in the back of his mind all day, and then discovered that he would have to go back down to the lobby if he wanted to pay for internet access. Instead, he opened up the file with the downloaded St. Germaine sessions and clicked on one at random that he hadn't watched yet, session seven. He jumped to about five minutes in.

On the screen, St. Germaine stood before a large blackboard on which nothing had yet been written. His hands were clasped and resting on the slight paunch of his stomach. He was speaking directly into the camera.

"...you see, there's coded information inside of me that, for some reason that no one has yet been able to determine, wants desperately to continue to exist. In order for it to continue to exist, at least for another eighty years or so, it needs to encode itself within a new human vessel. In order to produce a new human vessel, it needs me to achieve a certain physical state of affairs with a member of the opposite sex. The code's urge to survive is so strong, and its dominance over me so complete, that it's able to convince me that the best members of the opposite sex for me to achieve this state of affairs with are those with certain deposits of flesh around certain areas of their body, certain qualities of the bones in their face, even certain aromatic chemicals present in their breath. Of course, this was all before I met my wife."

He laughed before continuing.

"The point is that even though I'm able to see this very plainly, to see how beholden I am to this code and its will, I am not able to free myself from it, or even release myself from the delusion. The sight of an attractive female still elicits a certain pang in my chest, a certain primordial acknowledgement, a certain directive that demands to be immediately addressed. This is not a *thought* I have, but a feeling. And there's nothing I can do about it.

"Consider now that this is not merely some outside thing that we occasionally deal with. Nor does it only pertain to sex. It's stitched into the fabric of our very reality, this will that is not ours.

"Make no mistake: We are slaves to this code."

"Oh, enough," Oscar said into the stillness of the room. Reenergized now, he put his boots back on and went back down to the night clerk and paid $6.99 cash for the Wi-Fi code, which the clerk wrote on a Post-it note and slid across the desk to him along with his penny of change. The code was INTERNET.

Back upstairs he read the email standing with the laptop in his hand like the skull of Yorick.

Dear Oscar,
First allow me to say how surprised I was to see your message. My granddaughter set this account up for me some years ago, and it was only by happenstance that I recently

checked it. Generally speaking, I tend to prefer my privacy, but in this case I'm happy you were able to find me, even if the tidings you bore were ill ones.

I'm so terribly sorry to hear about your mother. Unfortunately, it's very important to me and my current students that I maintain strict confidentiality regarding the things that we discuss, even in death. I hope you understand, although I suspect that you may not. I will say, however, that Delia was a bright and loving person, and I will cherish her memory.

To answer your question, it's true that I have no formal degrees. So if, as you say, my premises don't lead to my conclusion, I must plead the ignorance of the blissfully unrigorous. In fact I would go so far as to suggest that you and I are hardly in the same field. I am not doing philosophy. I am simply helping people. "Seminars" then, as you've called them, is surely the wrong word—how about sermons?

Yours in sympathy,

Paul

Oscar considered an impulse to smash the laptop against the wall, and then tossed it onto the bed with disdain. Already composing a response in his head, he undressed and took a long shower, then got into bed, tried to think of nothing, and thought instead of his mother. *Would she be disgusted with this or would she understand?* It was a ridiculous question, with an obvious answer.

Oh Jesus, what am I doing here? He had, in the days immediately after her death, comforted himself with the idea that she was in heaven, where she could look down on him from time to time and smile in pride, but now he raced to remind himself that he did not *truly* believe in that kind of afterlife, could not believe in it no matter how much he would love to, and that his mother was not watching him, could not see what he was doing.

But he wasn't prepared to lose her in that way just yet. So he convinced himself that a properly perfect heaven would wield some discretion with regard to the earthly deeds that its inhabitants were able to view, and that she could hypothetically be there, enjoying all of its rewards, and still be blind to this situation specifically. *Thank God.*

When he awoke, the digital clock read 4:12. He reached over and switched off the alarm, which he had set for 4:30. He swung himself instantly out of bed and went to the window. The carpet was somehow cold. Outside in the parking lot, bathed in the light of the sodium lamps, a man leaned in toward the open driver's side window of an old Pontiac, yelling at the driver in a stage whisper, clearly upset but still considerate of those who were sleeping.

"She can have whatever she wants, but the bird stays with me," he was saying. "And you can call her right now and tell her I said that. She can even keep the cage. But the bird is mine!" The odd little scene was somehow charged with significance.

This will be a full day, Oscar thought.

As he got dressed (the same jeans and shirt as yesterday, new underwear and socks), Oscar found himself talking to his mother, which he supposed one would have to call a prayer, his lips moving very slightly and soundlessly as he thought the words.

Mom, I'm in a bad way here. This situation is not ideal and I'm sure you're not very proud of this but you see how I'm trying to do the best I can with what I've been dealt. I'm very scared, though. If you could just maybe ride along with me today, I think that would be a great help. Thanks, Mom.

He moved to the sink and dry heaved a few times, gagging, eyes watering, but nothing came up. He brushed his teeth staring at his own eyes in the mirror, a human male, age twenty-nine, height five foot eleven, weight one seventy-five, straight teeth, okay vision, slight stubble, in the year of our Lord two thousand and nine, standing right here in this weird sad place for the first and only time.

He spat, rinsed.

He still had three hours before what was supposed to happen but sleep was out of the question and there was nothing left to be done in the room, so he grabbed his bag and went to turn in the key card to the front office. The bearded man in his sixties behind the counter said they don't really ask for the keycards back but okay.

He drove to the gas station on the corner. As the pump fed the tank, he leaned against the hood and watched the sky lighten in the west and thought about how strange it was that he would ever have to die.

Stop it. He caught himself. *This is not the time for thoughts like that.* But he was beset with the feeling that everything, including both his personal environment and the universe in general, was so utterly ridiculous, a needless contrivance that would have been laughable if it wasn't so underpinned by misery and pain. A line of Schopenhauer returned to him, one that he had committed to memory as an undergraduate:

"Does it not look as if existence were an error the conse-
quences of which gradually grow more and more manifest?"
Once, he had found it funny.

He pulled into the first non-chain diner that he found,
trimmed in chrome and neon, and sat in a booth by the window and ate a stack of pancakes, two fried eggs on buttered
toast, and a side of bacon. He couldn't believe how much he
had been eating. He told himself he would compensate with
a light lunch.

Back on the road, riding as if in a trance. The sun rose.

Forty-five miles from the destination, still blindly following the GPS, he got off the highway and soon found himself
in some semblance of a town that showed only the slightest
signs of habitation. There were a few houses, half–blown-
down shacks behind chain-link fences, most with the parted-
out, rusted husk of a vehicle dead on the lawn of sand. They
seemed more like caves, features of the landscape that might
provide some shelter, rather than man-made additions to it.
The only human he saw was a pudgy child sitting on a concrete foundation slab tossing Skittles to a dog on a chain.

Oscar drove through the center of this town and came out
on the other side into an empty expanse of sagebrush that
stretched on for miles, over which three lines of sawtooth
mountains interlocked in the distance. He drove on this two-
lane road for fifteen minutes, encountering nothing except
a few trucks.

His adrenal glands were back into overdrive now, and he
pulled onto the shoulder to urinate. The desert soaked up his
water and in a few moments the ground at his feet was completely dry again.

It was eerily quiet out here. He could see the headlights of an approaching truck so far in the distance that they barely seemed to be moving at all. From the hard ground he dug out a fist-sized rock and threw it as far as he could into the brush. The dusty impact was clearly audible from twenty yards away.

This road turned into one that was smaller and less well paved. He drove through an open cattle gate and yet another road, smaller still, and Oscar couldn't tell if he was on private property now or not. Ahead, after a few more minutes, he saw what Dawn told him he would find: a tiny abandoned truck stop that looked like it hadn't been touched since the early fifties, before the interstate siphoned off all the traffic. He pulled into the parking lot under a red-lettered sign that read simply FOOD.

On one side of him, off about thirty yards, was the empty road. On the other side was an uninterrupted expanse of brush that dipped down toward the horizon. A great pall of dust, lit in the angled morning sun, hung over a brown sliver in the distance that Oscar realized after a moment must have been the country of Mexico.

It was 7:30, half an hour early. He shut off the engine and got out.

The little truck stop was boarded up, but half of the boards were missing. The interior was covered with indecipherable graffiti and broken glass. A line of swiveled diner stools still stood in the filthy shade, but the counter that was once in front of them had been taken away. Instead of going inside, Oscar sat down on a stone bench by the derelict gas pumps. A lizard scurried out from under his boots.

Sitting on the bench, he felt an unexpected stillness. He received some amorphous ideas about the absurdity of circumstance but was unable to pin anything down. He settled on: *Things could be so many different ways, but this is the way that they are.*

In a few minutes, off across the brush in the distance, there was some kind of disturbance, which he soon decided was a plume of dust. He watched it draw closer. It was hard to tell how far away it was: one mile? Five? He went back into the car and dug out the pack of cigarettes from the day before and lit one.

Oscar noticed that his hands, although they weren't quite shaking, were doing something weird, responding to something like coldness that moved in waves out from his center.

After a minute, a dot appeared at the base of the plume of dust. Slowly, it resolved into a helmeted man on an ATV, hauling ass, up on two feet like an equestrian to brace himself against the bumps in the ground. Oscar finished the cigarette and ground out the butt under his heel.

His phone rang, which startled him, and he looked at the incoming number: his father. *Shit,* he thought, and answered it.

"Dad, hi, it's actually a pretty bad time, what's up?"

It was a bad connection—he heard only several garbled consonants of his father's voice. He looked at the phone's display— just one bar of reception.

"Sorry Dad, I can't hear you—Dad! I'm gonna call you back in a little bit." He hung up.

The ATV was only a few hundred yards away now. He could hear its engine.

For the first time, he thought about guns. Didn't guns usually make appearances in scenes like this? A thousand movie scenes played before him. Would this guy have a gun on him? Should Oscar pretend like he had a gun? He saw the opening scene from *No Country for Old Men* in his mind, gut-shot narcos dying of thirst in the desert, a desert that hadn't looked too dissimilar from the one in which Oscar currently stood and in fact might not have been too far away.

That kind of thinking doesn't help anything, Oscar told himself. Either he was about to get shot or he wasn't. Too late now.

A minute later the man brought the ATV to rest in front of the Range Rover and dismounted. Instead of removing the helmet, he only flipped up the polarized visor. Blue eyes set in brown skin.

"A nice day for driving," the man said, his accented voice muffled in the padding of the helmet.

"You're the guy," Oscar said, because here he was, finally: the guy.

The man swung a backpack off his shoulders and handed it to Oscar. He flipped his visor down again, turned, and threw one leg back over the ATV.

Oscar couldn't stop himself.

"Wait," he said.

The man swiveled back around on the seat of the bike, both hands still on the handles.

"So…that's it?" Oscar said.

The man looked him over. Oscar saw himself in the reflection of the visor. "What else would there be?" he said, and gunned the throttle, taking off back across the desert in the direction from which he had come, back into the plume that hadn't even had time to settle, leaving Oscar standing there, dumbfounded.

He snapped back to life when he realized that he was now, officially, doing something exquisitely, almost unfathomably illegal. His head was a din of alarm bells. The pack, an olive green military-surplus thing, was heavy in his hands, seemingly filled to capacity. He knew he should probably check its contents but he couldn't bring himself to open the zipper. Instead he opened the empty trunk of the car, dug under the floor mat, and found the wheelwell for the spare tire. He nestled the pack, as gently as possible, into the space in the middle of the tire, and replaced the mat.

When he pulled out, the tires squealed.

By the time he made it back to the small town, his adrenaline was thrumming so bad that he began to feel like he might lose control of the car; his hands shook severely. He pulled over and gingerly lit a cigarette with quivering fingers. He tried to tell his body that physically speaking, everything was fine, that there was no need for a fight-or-flight response, but it refused to listen.

He got out of the car and did some stretches and jumping jacks to try to get some blood flowing and smooth out his nerves. From the run-down convenience store across the street he bought water and a pack of gum, and while he stood at the counter he realized that he might be on camera. He paid cash.

When he came back out, a woman in shorts and a Lakers jersey stood by the car. It was unclear where she had come from.

"Nice car, guy," she said.

Oscar got back behind the wheel without saying a word.

★ ★ ★

Going north, now carrying the package, Oscar's mind began to spin out different negative scenarios at a rate that astounded even him, until it gave up on specifics and began to simply broadcast a blanket of white-noise distress. Oscar tried on different mantras in an attempt to calm himself down and found that the most effective was something that returned to him from one of the St. Germaine tapes: *There is no such thing as a decision. There is no such thing as a decision.*

He felt his phone vibrate in his pocket, but he didn't reach for it. After thirty seconds, it vibrated again. The third time, he violated his promise to himself that he would not take his eyes off the road and fished it out of his pocket to look at the screen to see who was calling—his sister. A text from her popped up while he was looking at it.

Can you pick up? It's about Dad.

Oscar pulled into the parking lot of a Burger King and called her back. She picked up immediately.

"Hi, Oscar."

"This is not a very good time."

"I can't find Dad. His car is gone and I haven't seen him in two days."

"Two days?"

"Well, maybe more like a day and a half. But this is very unlike him. I'm worried. Where would he go? He's got no-where to go."

"He probably just went—yeah, actually, you're right. Did you check with the Andersons?"

"Haven't seen him."

"Okay. Well, it's early to be too concerned just yet. Keep calling around, maybe try his Knights friends, see if they know anything? I'm dealing with something that requires a lot of attention right now but I will call you back soon."

"Okay. I'll try to keep this terrible feeling at bay for now. Take care of yourself, please."

"I will."

He hung up and pulled back onto the road.

It was another hour before his brain alerted him to phenomena worth noting in his rearview mirror. Something about the way that the sun glinted off the grill of a car behind him by about half a mile reminded him of a way that he might have seen and failed to record the same glinting many miles and several exits earlier.

In another ten minutes, it was still there. For a while a truck came between them, but then it took an exit and the car, which Oscar thought he could now discern was black, remained, although it had dropped behind another quarter mile. Oscar decreased his speed by ten miles per hour to see if the car would gain on him, but it maintained the same distance.

As he drove, two narratives existed in parallel in Oscar's head: one in which he was being followed and one in which he wasn't. As strongly as he was able to argue with himself for the latter, the idea of the former was immediately the more vivid and compelling of the two possibilities, full of details about what would happen next. He applied slightly more pressure to the gas pedal and fled into the increasing traffic.

The road had grown back into a proper highway now, and

when he got off around noon to fill up the tank again at a large filling station, he first stopped and positioned the car so that he could watch the exit ramp. No black vehicle followed him off. And he didn't see anything that looked familiar while he took his time to walk around the tarmac and glimpse around the dumpsters to the far side of the Arby's.

You are being ridiculous, he told himself. *Keep it together. You're almost done.*

But then, back on the road twenty minutes later, he could swear he saw the car in the rearview again, only now he could tell that it wasn't a car but a pickup truck. It approached closer than it had been before, to no more than two hundred yards behind him. Oscar could make out three men sitting across the front.

Oscar experienced a new and unnamable terror. He felt some kind of clear, perfect perception, although perceiving nothing in particular. It was like looking through a powerful telescope at nothing but empty night sky with no stars, knowing that you are looking but knowing that you are looking at nothing. He told himself that this feeling was not doom.

He studied the men in the rearview for a moment. He could barely make out their three figures, just dots really, but he felt as if he was making eye contact with the one in the middle. Something clicked inside of him, and his paralyzing fear turned into a more useful form of a similar energy. He looked up to assess the traffic in front of him, said, "Fuck this," and hammered the accelerator.

The car took off like a rocket sled down the left lane.

Driving like he never had before in his life, Oscar wove through the handful of cars in his way and then got back in the left lane with a good straight stretch in front of him and opened it up. He watched the speedometer climb shockingly fast, eighty, ninety, and then one hundred. He had never driven one hundred before in his life. One hundred and one! *Jesus Christ!* It now felt not like he was driving a car, but like falling straight down, approaching terminal velocity.

Everything in the rearview fell away. His brain turned on rarely used centers of operation as it struggled to compete with the new pace of input. Oscar maintained this speed for a full five minutes, the cars in front of him bailing out of the left lane as they saw him hurtling closer to them. The engine was loving it, barely exerting itself, just hitting its stride.

"Yeah!" Oscar screamed at the smaller sedans as he passed. "Beat it!"

You should probably slow down.

The external world smeared into a blur and then began to fall away completely, beginning at the periphery as Oscar's field of focus narrowed into a smaller and smaller area ahead of him. The faster he went, the farther out in front of the car he had to cast his eye to gather information, assessing other cars and their positions and speeds when they were seemingly a mile away, and then bang, he passed them, and they ceased to exist. This was fun.

And then, at the exact instant that Oscar realized that this might not be the best idea even if he was being pursued, something worth noticing appeared in his rearview again. Red and blue lights.

Oscar's first thought was a mechanical one: *Well, that makes sense.* Then the rest flooded in: everything was already over, and it had hardly begun. *I guess this'll be it then*, he thought.

I made my play and it was looking okay for a minute there but now it's about to be over. There was more than a small amount of relief in the idea.

The cop had closed the distance with impressive speed and was on his tail before he could even move his foot from the accelerator to the brake. For one brief moment Oscar was struck with the simplicity of the notion that cops were not actually in physical control of your vehicle and that it was up to you to pull over when they asked you nicely with their lights, and that some people didn't. His speed climbed from 101 to 102.

Then his sinking rationality sent up a flare and he slowed down, which seemed to take around five miles, and pulled onto the shoulder, coming to rest like a meteor digging through steppe turf.

He laid his forehead against the top of the wheel and began the process of making peace with his new life in prison. He searched the glovebox for registration and found none. Bad start.

Oscar rolled down his window and waited.

In his rearview, the cop had his door open before his car had come to a stop. He marched toward Oscar's car furiously, shaking his head back and forth.

How would he explain that the car wasn't his? What would happen when they ran the plates? It had never been discussed. One of the edifices that Oscar had constructed to prop up this whole operation, namely that Dawn knew what she was doing, crumbled entirely.

And then, in the space of that two seconds when the cop was still approaching the car, about as slow as walking, the black truck passed on his right. Its three riders all had their heads turned toward him, looking. Time slowed down enough for Oscar to see the fray on the front of the vaquero hat worn by the one in the middle. It seemed as if he had enough time to make eye contact with all three of them, and then they were gone.

Back to his left, the officer was in his window.

"Are you fucking kidding me? You're just gonna blast past me like that? Make me run you down?" the cop said. He was in his thirties, skinny, face red partly due to complexion and partly to the anger that radiated off him in a brutish aura.

"Good morning, officer," Oscar said, and then by way of apology, "I...didn't see you."

"No, I suppose that you did not. But you see me now. License and registration."

"Here's my license. I...can't find the registration."

The officer smiled toothily, hand on hip, incensed and incredulous. He hadn't yet taken the license. "Well, where is it?"

"The car's not mine."

"Not yours."

"My friend's."

"Your friend okay with you driving his shiny new car damn near the goddamn speed of sound?"

"I guess not."

"Where you headed so fast?"

"I'm late for work."

"Oh yeah. And what line of work might that be?"

"I'm a professor of philosophy."

"I coulda sworn I thought you said 'work.'"

"It's a lot of grading. You'd be surprised."

"I didn't know they paid Range Rover money for that."

"Yeah, it's a friend's."

"You mentioned that. Well, ponder this for a second, Aristotle—you got anything in this nice fast car that I should know about?" He peered into the car, the front and then the back. "In fact, why don't you just go on ahead and step out of the vehicle, please?"

Here it was, the curtain rising on Oscar's fumbling production of deceit, his last act as a free man.

His mouth opened to produce a lie before his brain had fully formed it.

Some piece of communication gear chirped on the officer's shoulder and emitted an indecipherably urgent message in the voice of the dispatcher.

The cop didn't respond immediately but instead looked directly at Oscar, weighing his dislike for him and the desire to charge him with as much as possible against the urgency of this new development. The dispatcher squawked again; this time Oscar thought he heard the term "all units."

Still looking at Oscar, the cop pressed a button and acknowledged the call.

"You stay right here, you understand me? Someone else is coming for you. You don't go anywhere," he said as he turned and ran back across the dusty shoulder to his squad car.

"I'm not sure about the legality of that," Oscar said, but the cop had already slammed his door and peeled out hard into traffic with his lights and siren blaring.

Oscar sat there, looking forward, breathing heavily. What had just happened?

From where he was sitting, he could see the sign for the

next exit. On the GPS it looked to be about an eighth of a mile away.

He looked at the keys and wondered for a moment why the officer hadn't just taken them, and then turned them in the ignition.

As soon as he had pulled off the highway and driven down backroads for fifteen minutes he pulled to the side of the road near an empty field and called Dawn.

She picked up. "Your cell phone? Don't you watch movies? Go find a pay phone."

She hung up.

He drove on and found a pay phone outside of a convenience store in a strip mall a few miles away. He got out of the car, blipped it locked with the key fob, took a step away, and then turned and locked it again, double-checking.

He was surprised to hear a dial tone when he lifted the receiver to his ear. Looking through the plate glass into the store, he accidentally made eye contact with the cashier. Oscar turned his face away from him as he dug into his pants pockets for a quarter, dropped it into the slot, and dialed, reading the number that she had texted him off his cell.

"It's me," Oscar said.

"Sorry, I'm not one hundred percent sure it's a real thing, the cell phone thing, but it's better to play it safe."

"I almost just got arrested."

"Wait, what? Did you meet the guy? Do you have it?"

"Yeah, yeah, that part was okay. Are people following me?"

"Following you? Who?"

"I mean, do you think there's any reason why people would be following me?"

"No. I mean, shit, no, definitely no."

Oscar heard her muffle the receiver with her hand and whisper something to someone else in the room.

"I might be losing it a little bit," Oscar said.

"You're spooked."

"There were these three men, in a truck, and they were behind me for a while, and then when I sped up they were still there—"

"Is that it?"

"It's hard to explain. But I really think they were tailing me." Now that he was off the road, he wasn't so sure. It was hard to recapture the claustrophobic clarity of that moment.

"Listen to yourself. So people in a truck were behind you on the highway? Uh-oh, better freak out. You're being paranoid, which I don't blame you for, all things considered. But you're fine. Just get back here. Did you say you were almost arrested?"

"I came this fucking close, I swear."

"What happened?"

"Deus ex machina. Won't happen again."

"You need to relax. I can hear you breathing."

There was a silence. Oscar took three deep breaths, something his mother taught him to do when he was upset as a child.

"Mexicans?" Dawn asked, betraying a note of real concern.

"Yeah. I don't know. I guess."

"Well, it's not really saying much anyway."

"I'm still okay, right?" he said. "This is all still okay?"

"Everything is fine. You're overthinking it. Stop being a pussy. You haven't even crossed any borders. Just maybe stay off the highway for a little while until your head clears. Think of your family and hurry up and get back here. I'm hanging up now. Keep driving." She hung up.

Oscar turned around and sat down right on the curb. He felt like crying. The event was still too recent for him to fully comprehend how close he had come to being big-time arrested.

He felt like he was drowning. The air he breathed seemed not to be properly working on his lungs.

He tried to think about the money, about how it would feel when he cut his father a check and told his sister that he could help her out for a few months, if she needed it, while she figured out what she was going to do. But he found no motivating images. His imagination, as Sundeep would say, lacked any real robustness.

He dug in his pockets for the cigarettes and lighter. The pack was squashed, but he bent one cigarette back into shape. The lighter, however, had apparently vanished. He went into the store and bought another one and lit up as he walked back outside. He was starting to understand the appeal.

This was still navigable, he told himself back in the car, his hands finally beginning to slow their shaking. There was still a safe path out of here. The men who he thought were following him probably weren't. Maybe the cops had the license plate number of the car, that wasn't even directly connected to him, but maybe they didn't, and they only had him for speeding anyway. No reason to scramble the helicopters.

Still, though, being surrounded by various forms of oblivion on all sides was threatening to crack him up. He had been a criminal for all of four hours and was already coming apart. How were there people that did this regularly?

He tried to think like one of them, both to get into the mindset and to remind himself that, despite what it currently looked like, he in fact was not: *I am a criminal. I do what I want and get away with it. I make large amounts of money quickly and with comparatively small amounts of expended effort. I am a predator. I spare no thought for the safety or well-being of strangers. I am a bad man and I am fine with that. I think of little beyond ways to effect my own personal gain.*

This was enough to at least get him to turn the key in the ignition.

"Okay, be smart," he said. "Be smart."

Thinking now only of himself, he realized that Dawn, in her desire to get her hands on the bag that was currently wedged into the wheelwell, might have been incorrect in her advice to get back ASAP. He felt that he needed to stay off the highway for a little while, partially to regain his composure and partially to let some of the hypothetical heat on the part of the police, who might or might not be looking for him, dissipate, if in fact that was really something that happened, if the concept of *heat* was a real concept at all.

Driving again, he continued roughly northward along backroads for another thirty minutes, with his eyes held on the rearview mirror as much as through the windshield. His body felt battered by his nerves—his neck seized in pain from the tension and he had trouble turning his head. When he no longer felt sun on his skin, he realized suddenly that he was in a forest of great natural beauty, with redwoods towering over the winding road on either side.

He came out of these woods and pulled into an empty scenic overlook situated above an enormous lake. He stepped out of the car and tried to massage his neck. "Please," he said to his body. "Come on." He sat on the guardrail and smoked another cigarette and watched a boat describe a white V of wake into the lake far below him, the lowering sun carpeting the water in gold. *Well, this is nice,* he allowed himself to think, until another car pulled onto the gravel and he nearly fell over backward.

Walking briskly back to the car with his head lowered, he received a text from Sundeep:

Dude, squash?

To which he replied:

Can't, busy

He continued north, stopping to replot his course every time that the GPS insisted he get back on the highway. Eventually he zoomed the map out to check the distance back to the university and figured that at this pace, driving on backroads under the speed limit, his heart might give out under stress before he ever made it home.

So when it got dark, he merged back on the highway, stayed in the right lane, and maintained his non-suspicious speed. He dropped the mantra of criminality that had been running in his head nonstop since he had seized on it and even allowed himself to listen to NPR, but the dulcet tones of the news program did nothing to soothe him, as they usually did.

He had been operating at such a high gear all day that around 8:00 p.m. he felt as if he had been awake for forty-eight hours rather than sixteen. He nodded off twice behind the wheel, one time swerving severely into the shoulder, before he admitted to himself that he would not be sleeping in his own bed that night and that he was going to have to get that figured out.

He stopped at the next roadside motel, a national chain. He would close his eyes for two, maybe three hours, and then get back on the road. In the little main office, he was given a card to fill out, which had spaces for all kinds of info, including his license plate number.

"Oh, jeez, I can never remember this," Oscar said, over-acting for the girl behind the counter. "Let me go back out and check."

With his body beginning to crash, he got back in the car and immediately back on the highway and drove another twenty-five miles until he saw from the road another, even shittier looking place called The Villa. A room was half the price and they didn't ask him a single thing.

Back in another motel room, again on the second floor, again overlooking a parking lot that was like something Hopper might have painted on a day that he was feeling particularly depressed, again sitting on a bed that had been both witness and accomplice to who knows how many decades of various horrors, sexual and otherwise. From a room adjacent in an indeterminate direction it sounded as if someone was giving someone else a buzz cut in the bathroom. Now that he was sitting on the bed, going to sleep seemed absurd.

On the floor by the door were two bags, one that belonged to him and one that didn't. He knew that he was going to have to open the latter one, to lay his eyes on whatever mysteries waited inside, to make sure he wasn't just smuggling sawdust. Maybe a bunch of plastic snakes on springs would burst forth, and he would call Dawn and she would laugh and laugh. *We got you so good!* she would say. *You sounded so scared!*

But instead he opened the other bag, the one that belonged to him, and pulled out his laptop.

He wanted to send St. Germaine the email that he had now fully drafted in his head, but here there was not even the option to pay for Wi-Fi. In fact, he thought, groups of students could take a tour of this room to get a sense of what it was like to be alive in 1992; the insectile convexity of the television screen, the bulk of the yellowed-plastic phone, the insane teal pattern of the carpet. *Why didn't I bring a book with me?*

Oscar realized for the first time how colossally stupid it was for him to even bring his laptop, just so that he could read an email. But then again, the bitter anger he felt when he saw St. Germaine on the screen had sustained him well and clarified his focus. That's why he had been watching them slowly: he didn't want to build up a tolerance. Plus, he recalled, Dawn had told him not to think, and he was good at following directions.

He keyed up one of the PSG videos and clicked the progress bar past the intro and left it paused, St. Germaine frozen on the screen leaning forward, with his mouth halfway open and his eyes mid-blink, looking palsied or possessed.

Oscar had at first thought that to watch all of the tapes would be to implicitly grant St. Germaine a legitimacy that Oscar had quickly decided he didn't deserve. There was no reason to try to develop an understanding of the entire system when it was clear that St. Germaine didn't seem to put too much thinking behind it himself. But Oscar could admit to himself now that he was beginning to understand. The man was a charlatan and a thief, an abuser of the weak, and his "work," if it could even be called that, was based on nothing that could ever be accused of being a properly presented fact.

But still, there was something there. Perhaps it was merely the allure of showmanship, or the respect demanded of true conviction. Once, while Oscar was riding the L during a visit to Chicago, a raving preacher dressed in tatters stepped onto the train and began a nonsense sermon. Oscar could sense the other riders turning away and trying to block the man out, but Oscar listened to every word, secretly fascinated, as he explained the causes of the coming apocalypse, which had something to do with a stuffed elephant that he carried under his arm. Oscar thought that if he listened closely enough, he could sketch the outlines of the underlying logic and find some common reality with this man. In fact, it seemed terribly important. The man had tears in his eyes—he was trying to save their *lives*. And nobody cared to see if he was telling any truth.

Maybe the real reason Oscar hadn't watched all of the tapes was out of fear that they might start to make sense.

He hit Play. St. Germaine resumed the point that he had been making.

"You are an animal. Please understand this."

Oscar hit Pause.

He got the bag that wasn't his and sat with it on the bed like nervous prom dates. It certainly had heft.

He unzipped the large main compartment and saw what was inside.

Here in his hands was the proof that everything was exactly as it seemed. The bag of drugs was nothing other than a bag of drugs. This had all been real.

Dawn had refused to tell him the specifics of what he would be picking up beyond allowing that it was a fair quantity of illegal but not particularly immoral or physically ruinous drugs, which he assumed meant cocaine, but he never imagined that it could possibly be this much. Inside the bag were four large, soft brick shapes, each about the size of a ream of printer paper, wrapped in duct tape. He didn't have to be a DEA agent to know they would weigh exactly one kilo each.

In this moment, Oscar doubted not only the spasm of bad decisions that had led him to this horrible ordeal, but also every decision he had ever made in his life: the decision to leave home, the decision to eschew the pursuit of money over all else, the decision to try to be truly smart, the endless hours he had spent in pursuit of perception.

He tried to return to his "I am a criminal" mantra to stem the rising tide of panic in his chest, but saw immediately that he would not be able to suppress it. He was seized with a single instinct, which was to get as much space as possible between himself and the contents of this bag.

A thought intruded, elbowing through the urge: *You can flush it.* And then *you need to flush it. Flush it and tell Dawn you lost it, or sold it, or it was stolen, or to do her worst and go fuck her-*

self but that she had chosen the wrong man for the job and he would
rather take his chances with professional disgrace and financial ruin
than bear this thing for another mile. Hell, flush it and go tell the
cops yourself, see if her safeguards are as strong as she thinks.

Confident that he was finally thinking clearly, and forc-
ing to the periphery of his thoughts the threats of physical
violence and the promise of monetary salvation for his family, he dragged the bag into the tiny bathroom and sat down
on the floor at the foot of the toilet. He knew that this was
a bad idea, but it was nested under so many other bad ideas
that he wasn't even sure what that meant at this point. All he
could think about was how good it would feel to be safe again.

He didn't have a knife, so he produced his key ring and
found the sharpest one, the small key to his book locker in
the school library. He began to saw away at the middle of the
duct tape of one of the bricks until a small hole developed. As
the bag flexed, it exhaled tiny puffs of white powder, which
landed on Oscar's hands and immediately made him feel filthy.

Finally, he held the brick over the water of the bowl and
thrust the key so that he could begin a lateral disembowel-
ing cut. Some of the powder wafted out, like from a pitch-
er's rosin bag.

The key clicked against something hard buried in the
brick's middle.

Hmm?

He brought the brick bag to his lap and poked around a
bit more and confirmed that there was indeed something inside that was not powder. He worked the hole that he had
made until it was about an inch long and he could get his
fingers inside.

What he pulled out was another smaller ziplock bag that contained within it some kind of small electronic device.

Intrigued now, Oscar set the brick down on top of the other three and brought the device to the small desk and turned on the lamp. It was a little bit larger than one inch square, made of gray plastic, with a small battery compartment and something that looked almost like—an antenna.

Oh.

Oscar jumped, fumbled for the lamp switch, couldn't find it, and ripped the cord out of the wall. Then he dove across the bed to turn out the overhead and frantically lowered the blinds. He double-checked that he had locked the dead bolt and fed the nut on the feeble little brass chain into its slot.

In the dark, taking care to make no noise, he went back to the desk and examined the device by the light of his shitty cell phone, which, he noted, was at 20 percent power.

Now that he was looking at things on their face, he did not attempt to convince himself that this thing was anything other than a tracking device of some sort.

It was indeed quite possible, he told himself, *that I am being followed.* Actually, he was just going to go ahead and mark that one down as a definite. It was quite possible that he had been followed to this place. It was quite possible that his hypothetical followers were watching this room currently.

He went to the window and raised the level of the blinds to one millimeter above the sill so that he could kneel on the floor and look out at the parking lot. All seemed still. Passing light from the highway was visible over a small embankment on the other side of the lot, where arc lights illuminated a sad menagerie of cars that stood in contrast to his expensive, overdesigned SUV.

Although he was able to look at his situation truthfully, he was not yet prepared to decide on a course of action, and so he stayed like this, on his knees, forehead pressed against the fabric of the blinds, for some time. After what felt like an hour but was probably more like ten minutes, he found that he was praying.

Dear God, dear Mom, Uncle Steven who died in a helicopter in Vietnam, please help me, please help me, please help me...

His eyes closed.

After another indeterminate amount of time, something either without or within him caused them to open. Then, as he watched, a black pickup truck, *the* black pickup truck, pulled into the lot and parked. Its lights shut off.

Oscar noted with some degree of happiness that he did not feel particularly scared, perhaps because his capacity for fear had been pushed past a certain threshold beyond which further increases failed to register. Or, better stated, he was scared, he was fucking terrified, but he wasn't paralyzed.

He crawled on his knees (for some reason this felt safer than standing, even though the blinds were closed), and grabbed the device and lay down with it on the floor next to the bed. From outside he thought he heard car doors shut.

He propped his phone up on its side and in the anemic light of its screen fumbled with the battery door on the strange device. He slid it open with his thumb and detached the D battery from the wire clip.

Back at the window peering through the slit in the blinds, he could make out three slim figures, dark with shadow, conferring by the hood of the truck. One of them held something in his hand that glowed, either a phone or something with a screen, and he gestured with it toward the building, sweeping it from end to end. The figure in the middle, the tallest one who wore the hat that Oscar had noticed earlier on the road, shook his head, and then said something to the third, and then turned back to the first and prodded him in the chest with his finger.

As Oscar watched them, they seemed to come to some sort of conclusion. As they began to move toward the building, they were swept for an instant in the headlights of a turning car and he could see their clothes—jeans, boots—but not their faces. They passed down out of Oscar's vision into the row of doors on the first floor.

Oscar couldn't think. Tried his limbs and couldn't move. He felt sweat form on the back of his legs.

A minute later, by looking sideways out of the extreme edge of the window, he could see an arm appear at the top of the stairs at the end of the second floor's outdoor hallway. A veined hand and forearm below a rolled-up white sleeve— that's all the angle would allow him to see. The hand extended a finger and pointed down the hall.

Oscar lowered the blinds completely and lay down on his stomach on the opposite side of the bed from the door. He could hear footsteps approaching slowly from down the hall, but he did not hear the men say anything to each other. He felt his heartbeat against the floor like hammer blows and had the momentary terror that it could be heard out in the hall and would give him away like a scent.

The sound of their footsteps passed from the left of the door and moved down to the next room to the right, stopped there, and then returned two rooms back to the left. The sounds of softly spoken Spanish followed. Oscar couldn't pick out any words.

They were now standing directly outside his door. He could hear six feet and the weight they carried.

He felt their presence like a fire, sucking the oxygen out of the room through the crack under the door. Peripheral sounds died away. The whirr of the fan, the tiny hum of the fluorescent lights, the buzz of the ice machine outside were all muted as the world seemed to pause for an inhalation in the moment before the window would shatter or the door would come flying in off its hinges.

There was a tiny knock at the door.

It was so quiet that Oscar had trouble believing what he'd heard. Perhaps it was just a creaking of a floorboard. He focused on the feel of the carpet against his face, tried to burrow down into it as if it were soft black sand, clung to it like a vertical rock face. Outside, he heard three voices' worth of harsh whispers.

Then he heard the footsteps recede down the hall toward the stairs.

When Oscar worked up the nerve to open his eyes, peel himself from the floor, and crack the blind again, either a minute or an hour later, the truck was gone.

He slumped down with his back against the door. His heart was more whirring than beating. He tried to take a few deep breaths.

He picked up the receiver of the room's phone and dialed

Dawn. It rang four times and went to her voice mail. He hung up and texted her from his cell:

Fucking pick up.

He called back immediately.

"Where are you," she said.

Oscar spat out in a whisper, "It's real. I saw them again. They were just here."

"Where's here?"

"A motel somewhere. I don't even know."

"What's happening?"

"Those guys, those same three guys, they followed me here. They were just standing right outside the door a second ago. There was a...a...tracking device in the bag. I found it before they showed up, otherwise they would have known exactly where I was. What do you know about that? Why would there be a tracking device?"

"Ah—okay. A device?"

"You need to admit to me that you don't know what you're doing. You've never taken on this much before. You've never dealt with this element before. You sent me out here because you weren't sure if you were going to get fucked and now here you are, getting fucked, and I'm getting it worse."

"I know what I'm doing."

"Bullshit."

"You need to stay there. I'll send Ramos."

"No way. Too far. And even if I waited, what then? Ramos covers my escape with a hail of gunfire?"

"I don't think he actually owns a gun."

"A hail of vague threats?"

There was silence on the other end of the line.

"Guess what else?" he said. He had mapped out in advance exactly none of this conversation.

"What?"

"I want forty thousand."

"Wha—"

"I want forty thousand or I walk out of this room with this bag held above my head and hand it over on a silver fucking platter. On the world's biggest coke mirror."

"You wouldn't do that."

"I wouldn't? Dawn, who do you think I am?" He was yell–whispering now. "You think I'm handling this well? You think I'm not close to the edge of reason? I am not supposed to be here. I am a fucking METAPHYSICIAN! You dragged me down out of an ivory fucking TOWER!"

"Okay, okay. Forty. Jesus."

"Fine. Good."

"What are you going to do?"

He hung up.

17

The clock read 2:15 a.m. He had only closed his eyes briefly, but for some reason, he felt completely rested, although perhaps it was just that his adrenal glands had had a proper recovery period and were now once again firing full force. He stuffed the hole he had made in the brick with a hand towel from the bathroom to stop any of the powder from escaping, returned all four bricks to the bag, slung it over his shoulder along with his own bag, and headed for the door.

He would drive without stopping to get to the university in the morning (the thought occurred to him that if he found himself beginning to nod off that he was particularly well supplied to self-medicate), drop the bag at Dawn's feet, receive the money from her if she actually had it but to be honest at this point he barely cared, and then go back to his room, sit down, maybe cry, and grade papers for the rest of his life. He fantasized briefly about this scene: no obligations, no concerns, no thoughts at all other than how to properly illustrate to a freshman that her conclusions did not follow from her premises.

There were just a few more hours of road between him and his desk. All thoughts of pussying out had passed from him, like a fever.

Outside all was still. The night had grown cool.

He bounded down the stairs and jogged to the car and blipped it unlocked. He threw both bags into the passenger seat as he jumped up behind the wheel. He reached for the ignition with the key in his right hand while his left hand began to close the door but then there was another hand on the door holding it open and Oscar saw a nickel-plated hand-gun pointed at him and a voice was saying *relax, relax, relax.*

"Give me the keys," the voice said from somewhere above the gun.

Oscar gave the voice the keys.

"You don't have a gun," the voice said.

"No," Oscar said.

The hand without the gun patted at Oscar's pockets, his waistband, his rib cage.

"Okay. Buckle up. I'm going to come around and get in."

Oscar buckled his seat belt. The door was shut. The man walked around the hood of the car, passed through the head-lights. He wore a white button-down shirt tucked into his Wranglers, the big black vaquero hat covering his face.

As Oscar watched the man pass through the headlights, he felt the bottom of his own soul drop out, shards of himself spill downward into a freezing chasm, and the cold rush in. This was something new.

"Okay then," the man said as he moved the bags down

onto the floor and got into the passenger seat. He looked up at Oscar and smiled at him. His teeth were very white. "Boy, I didn't think it would be that easy, just waiting in the dark. I thought I might be there all night." He spoke with only a slight accent.

Oscar couldn't believe the simplicity, the dumb weight of his own foolishness.

"I thought you were gone," Oscar said, like a child.

"No. Right over there behind that tree. You found the tracker, didn't you, huh?"

The man rested his hat on his knees. He looked to be in his early forties, light brown skin, with lines only beginning to hint at themselves in his face. His jet-black hair hung to his neck. He thumbed at his phone with the hand that didn't hold the gun, pecking out the letters of a text message.

The automatic dome light went off and the car was dark. Nothing stirred in the parking lot. About a hundred yards away, which might as well have been ten miles, a skinny woman in a tank top walked a small dog in the gravel that lined the sidewalk outside of the rooms.

"What's happening now?" Oscar eventually said.

"Now we're waiting. What's your name?" The man was almost jovial. He sat in the passenger seat with the detached self-interest of a driving instructor.

Oscar tried to think of a fake name that would sound convincing and came up with nothing, not one name, a complete blank. "I don't want to tell you."

"We're going to be looking through your wallet in a little bit."

After a moment, Oscar said, "Oscar," and the man smiled.

"Like the grouch!" he said. "Oscar, hombre, I really just cannot believe that that tree thing worked. You had us huffing and puffing for a while there, huh? This car can *fly*. Wouldn't expect it, by the size. And then all I do is sit down behind a tree and you come jogging into my arms. What's your last name?"

"Boatwright."

"Boatwright? The fuck kind of name is that?"

"My people used to make boats. A long time ago. At least, probably."

"And now you do this shit," he said, meaning run around with drugs eluding armed men.

"Not regularly."

The man turned his attention to the bag at his feet. He unzipped it and sucked some air over his teeth when he saw what was inside.

"Well, *damn*, Oscar! Look at this. You were going to be rich, huh?"

Oscar stayed silent. The man turned his attention back to him. He looked him up and down.

"Oscar, I gotta ask," the man said, in full mock-congeniality now. "What are you doing out here? I mean you specifically. Not many gringos in this line of work, and the ones that are, all meth'd out, shitty beard, no teeth, Pantera T-shirt."

"I'm not quite sure," Oscar said. "It was out of my control."

"Well, you really ought to be sure. I can't recommend this life for guys like you. Because now you're thinking, well, shit, this was a bad idea, here I am in a car with a gun in my face, and who is this wetback and what does he have planned for me?"

"I wouldn't use that word," Oscar said.

"I can tell already that you're a good person. What's this here?"

He picked up the crumpled note that Dawn had left to Oscar on the dash about the GPS, with the Xs and Os.

"Hugs and kisses? Oh my God, man, you never had a chance!" He laughed and slapped his knee with the hand holding the gun. With his left hand he hit power on the GPS and zoomed out until he saw the route's destination. "And so far from home!"

The man extracted a cigarette from his breast pocket and lit it and when he turned back to Oscar, a change had come over his face. He kept his eyes on Oscar.

Oscar looked straight out through the windshield, watching an empty Doritos bag revolve in the breeze on its way across the parking lot. Cool Ranch, he noted with a pang of absurdity that threatened to either make him burst into laughter or tears.

"Honestly, Oscar, you seem a bit too calm. Usually at this point there's crying, begging, things like this. Let's be clear about something. In Juarez I used to make a man kill his own wife before killing him. Put the gun in his hand and hold it up to her head for him, and bang. Make him drown his children. And this was not a long-ago period of my life. Men like me, it's about reputation, so these things are important."

Oscar figured that the other two men, who couldn't have gone far, were now on their way back to pick them up and take them somewhere, and that was as far into the future as he dared guess at. An epistemic horizon, the term occurred to him, and he was trying desperately to keep it as near to him as possible.

"You didn't tell me your name," Oscar said.

"That's right, I didn't," the man said. He took a drag on his cigarette, and Oscar felt the first nascent pangs of a yearning for nicotine.

"Ha! Just kidding. What a fake tough guy thing to say. I wouldn't normally tell you, but it's interesting. My surname is Matadamas. Do you know what that means? I assume you have no Spanish. 'Lady killer.' You believe that shit? And yet I've never killed a woman. You ever build a fucking boat?"

"I thought you just told me about killing someone's wife."

"I told you that I made *him* do it."

In the dim relief cast by the sodium lights, Oscar saw old acne scars on Matadamas's face. His face had regal features, and implied an interesting long-arc story and layered internal states. Oscar struggled to divine some kind of intent from his expression but came up with nothing.

"How does this business work?" Oscar said, trying to sound resigned and yet fascinated by his fate, which regarding the latter, he actually was. But there was still a slight element of resistance that he didn't want to betray: the thought that every second that he could keep this guy talking was another second that he wasn't being murdered.

"You seem smart," Matadamas said. "I bet you could figure it out."

"My guess is that you bribe someone along the chain of commerce to bug a—I don't know the term—shipment? And then you pick it off when it's easiest."

"More threaten than bribe. And it's almost never this easy," Matadamas said, a grin on his face that might have been mistaken for friendly.

"And you don't just do it in Mexico because—"

"Because then I'd have to get it across the border myself. So thanks for that." He flicked his cigarette butt out the window, extracted another from his shirt pocket and lit it, bringing the lighter up in his right hand, which still held the gun.

"Oscar, can I tell you a story? I want to tell you a story," Matadamas said, taking a drag. He looked out into the darkness. Oscar watched his expression soften with memory.

"When I was a boy I had a younger brother and sister. My family was poor. My mother washed other people's laundry and my father did not exist. You see the picture? It's common enough. We had a tin roof, dirt floor, all that shit."

"This was in Juarez?" Oscar said, still preternaturally eager to please, engage as an active listener, even at gunpoint.

"No. A different place. When I was ten years old my mother took up with a man who owned a store and had a little money and so he thought he owned us, too. He would hit my mother and do other things. Our walls were so thin that I could hear everything. What he told her to do, how to bend. He would hit me, for nothing, for being in the room, for being in the world. He would hit my siblings. He was a big fat man."

Matadamas's phone chirped and he stopped to peek out a response. He returned the phone into one of his chest pockets and continued.

"But I was only ten. What can you do? I would lay awake and hear him with my mother in the other room, plugging my ears. I couldn't do shit. In the morning, my mother would have a black eye, and there he was drinking coffee at the table.

"Six years I lived like this. Six years of listening for the sound of his boots so that I could hide under my bed. Six years of my mother hiding her bruised face with makeup. Six years, no power. And then one day I woke up and looked in the mirror and I had grown. I was tall. I had muscles. I had hair on my balls.

"And then another day soon after that, the fat man, whose name was Juan, decided that my mother had grown too old and he turned his eyes on my sister, who was twelve. I was behind the house trying to fix a motorbike. He didn't know I was home. I heard the sounds coming from the window."

Headlights from the road swept the car and Matadamas's face was briefly illuminated. He took a drag on the cigarette and looked Oscar in the eyes.

"Think for a second. Imagine it. See yourself there—the dusty ground and puddle of motor oil, the heat of the sun, the screams coming from inside. Feel the years bubbling up, boiling over. Feel it? You are glowing from head to toe, like steel in a forge. Now imagine how good it is to pick up that torque wrench, go into that room, see him with his back turned, fumbling with his belt over your beautiful little sister, to already know what was going to happen next and that it was going to happen because of you, that you and only you were the one that was going to make it happen. Everything is perfect. You feel like some kind of saint. The first time you hit a human body with something metal and feel the bones move around deep inside, get all messed up? That's something you don't forget."

He curled the fingers of his left hand up into a C, as if it wasn't the slender handle of a revolver he was holding but rather a hefty wrench.

"I started with his knee, because I thought I was just going to stop him, get him to the ground. But he went down in a pile and turned to look at me, and I saw that he knew what I knew before I knew it."

Matadamas paused. Oscar understood his role here.

"What'd you do then?" he said.

"The fuck you think I did? I sent my sister out of the room and fucking killed him dead as shit. First I messed his legs up though. We lived outside of town so there was nobody to hear him. Then I stuffed his body into an oil drum and buried him out in the desert where he's been ever since, under a pile of stones and four feet of dry dirt, while I enjoy my life and go about on all sorts of adventures on the surface of the earth. Last time I was home, I went and pissed on him."

"Why are you telling me this?" Oscar said, although he had an idea.

"Because it's the best thing I ever did and I like to tell it whenever I can."

Oscar thought then, for the first time for real, that he was probably going to die. He was Matadamas's confessor, meant to take some of his guilt with him up to the gallows.

Here was that absurdity again. *Die? Me? What?*

Matadamas looked at the time on his phone.

"Just maybe a few more minutes," he said.

Oscar started to cry. He tucked his chin into his chest.

"What's this now?" Matadamas said.

"I'm sorry. My mother died recently."

Matadamas nodded. "Ah, yes. We're tough guys but it's okay to miss your mother."

"Also I don't want to die."

"This is another thing that you hear frequently. Well, you've so far given us no reason for me to make it take any longer than it needs to."

Matadamas flicked his second cigarette butt out the window, went in to his pack to retrieve another one, and found that it was empty.

"I have more in my bag," Oscar said.

"Well, gracias there, Oscar."

Matadamas leaned down to open Oscar's bag with his left hand and tugged on the zipper, but it snagged.

Oscar wondered, if he was going to be given an opportunity to save himself, would it be soon? It would have to be soon. But how would he know?

For some reason, a random image saved in some deep-storage synapse returned to him from many years ago, that he hadn't remembered in a decade. In the memory he was eight. There had been some confusion between his parents; both of them, it turned out later, had thought the other was going to pick Oscar up from the chess club that he attended in the auxiliary gym of a local Catholic church every Tuesday and Thursday afternoon over that summer.

The administrator was supposed to watch each kid until they were picked up, but when all who remained were Oscar and another boy who was famous for his odd smell, Oscar became worried that he would have to follow this teacher down empty halls to an office somewhere, where a yellow rotary phone sat for the almost exclusive use of forgotten un-picked-up children, and he would have to work his way through the various phone numbers that he had memorized for these situations. He might even have to call and explain to Mrs. Anderson from up the road, around whom he was uncomfortable, and beg her to come pick him up and drive him the nine miles home.

This ordeal, for whatever reason, seemed just simply entirely undoable, and although he didn't know how he would get home otherwise, he slipped away from the teacher when she had her head down in a paperback, and watched from behind a bush as the other kid's dad pulled up in a teal station wagon and opened the door for his son, and the teacher looked up, saw that there were no more children around her, assumed she had completed her job satisfactorily, locked the door behind her, and drove off in her own car. And so Oscar returned to sit at the top of the large stone steps all by himself, waiting, as the late afternoon turned to twilight and the fireflies rose up out of the lawns to laze in the cooling air.

Matadamas laid the gun down on his knee so he could use both hands to open the bag.

Oscar found it funny that now, so many years later, he had the vocabulary to describe the feeling of the memory to himself; it was tinged with a sense of dawning, unexpressed calamity. Just how much trouble was he in? Was his mother about to turn the corner in the Seville, her eyes red with tears, begging the forgiveness of her only son from out the window before the car had even stopped? Or had she maybe taken to her bed with one of her episodes, and was his father working late, so that Oscar's absence wouldn't even be noted for hours? Would he have to walk? Could he make it home before the coming of the full dark that lands on Indiana like a closing cellar door? These were the only possibilities he could imagine, just these few, and yet the world was so, so full of them.

They surrounded him, waiting to be born. How he had gotten home that day, he could no longer remember.

Oscar lunged and grabbed for the gun with two hands.

Matadamas got a hand on it before Oscar could pull it away and the cab filled with light for an instant and Oscar was deafened by a popping sound that he felt do something to the air around his face. The window to his left exploded outward and glass tinkled down around his shoulders.

When he next realized what was happening, he saw that he was holding the gun, and even pointing it at Matadamas's belly. His ears rang painfully.

"Keys," he said.

Matadamas seemed more perplexed than surprised. "Well, this I do not believe."

"Keys!" Oscar screamed, gesturing with the gun as if it was a leash attached to a dog that he wouldn't be able to control much longer.

"Just relax—you're shaking. Relax your finger or it will go off," Matadamas said and took the keys from his jacket pocket and placed them on the dashboard. A light flicked on in a room of the motel.

"Now, out."

"Oh my God," Matadamas said, eyes wide in rage, reaching slowly for the door handle. "You're already dead."

"I'm acting out of fear, which is dangerous for us both. I think I should probably shoot you but I'm going to let you get out of the car."

Matadamas opened the door, and after one look into Oscar's eyes that seemed for an instant almost intrigued before darkening, he dropped down and sprinted out over the boundary of the parking lot and into the night. Oscar grabbed the keys, fumbled them into the ignition, and was back on the highway in thirty seconds. One mile later, going in the opposite direction on the other side of the median, a police cruiser hauled ass, sirens blaring.

"What the fuck, what the fuck, what the fuck," Oscar repeated to himself over and over, out loud. The gun lay pointed barrel-down in the cupholder. He couldn't bring himself to touch it or even move it out of view. He used his left elbow to knock out onto the road the little gems of glass that still clung to the window. Eventually, he picked up the gun with two fingers like it was something contaminated and jammed it underneath the driver's seat as deeply as he could reach without taking his eyes off the road.

The sky lightened and then suddenly there was the sun although he had not seen it rise. The rest of the drive home passed without incident.

18

"Whoa," Dawn said when she opened the door.

"I haven't really slept," Oscar said. He had avoided his reflection and so he didn't know what he looked like, but he had never felt so bleary and exhausted in his entire life. He dragged his spirit behind him on the ground like a tangled parachute. The bag was slung over his shoulder. It was sometime in the afternoon.

"Is that it, right there?" Dawn said to him, looking at the bag. "Wow. Come in."

There was no one else inside. He put the bag down on the kitchen counter. Dawn locked the front door behind him and closed the blinds that covered the sliding glass door that led to the back steps. Slowly, she opened the bag and removed its contents, stacking the four bricks on top of one another, like bulging reams of printer paper.

"Holy moly," she said. She was wearing a bathrobe over jogging shorts and a university T-shirt.

"You should have told me it was going to be this much," Oscar said.

"You would have never gone." Dawn still looked at the stack of bricks, her eyes tinged with reverence. She hefted one of the bricks like a chicken at the grocery store, feeling its weight.

"You must have been worried," he said.

"About you or the...this?" she said.

"I was talking about that," he said, pointing. "But now I maybe think that you were worried about me, too."

"I think you underestimate yourself. I was never worried."

"Hey. Guess fucking what. There was a gun pointed at me. It went off actually. This is the first thing I should have mentioned. Your window is broken."

"Wait, really? That's okay about the window. A gun?"

"There were probably three of them, actually. There were three guys. Just like I told you."

"Do they know where to find us?"

"Maybe? I have no idea." He reached into his pocket and tossed the tracking device, without its battery, onto the counter.

Dawn set down the brick. "What the hell is that?"

"I guess you thought I was hallucinating or something."

A change came over Dawn's face. "This could be an issue for sure," she said.

Oscar noticed for the first time their closeness. Dawn's eyes found his and then moved away.

"What is your deal?" Oscar said.

"What?"

"Admit that you were worried about me."

"Fine! All right. Jeez."

"All right what?" Oscar asked.

"All right I was worried about you! What an asshole."

Oscar pulled her to him and kissed her. It was long enough that he had enough time to think, *Well! Look what's happening now.* And then he pulled away.

"I swear to Christ you almost got me killed," he said.

"But you're fine. We will deal with it. And now we're rich."

This time she kissed him.

Physical memories returned to him: the way her body responded to his. The way her energy unspooled around him and recoiled just when he thought he could interpret it.

Her bathrobe was discarded on the kitchen floor, next to one of his boots, the other in the hall leading to her bedroom near his Piggly Wiggly shirt. Her room was dark, bed unmade, window fan running, blinds already drawn.

They coupled quickly, as if to sneak the act by one another. At one point, with her on top of him, Oscar had the sudden thought, *I should be dead!* and he was afforded a moment to perceive how much he preferred the current arrangement of things. He even obtained some distance from the essentially empty descriptors that he used at all times to regard himself: professor, son, brother, moral actor, not a genius academic but a diligent journeyman, unwealthy, still largely screwed. For a moment he fell away from, or was lifted out of, these ideas, into a space where some unstrippable part of himself could exist unalloyed.

Afterward they both were silent. Oscar lay down next to her, too tired to feel awkward or out of place. He had entered a new realm of fatigue, something that felt like a good kind of death, a complete emptying rather than a burdening. The last thought he had before he fell asleep was that if the person he thought he was differed considerably from the person that he actually was, he would never know it. When he closed his eyes, he saw road.

When he awoke, the clock on Dawn's nightstand said 2:15 p.m.

"Wow," he said.

Dawn was still next to him. She opened her eyes.

"Did you have class today?" he said.

"Did you?" she said.

He laughed. "How are your grades?"

"Great."

"That's good."

She moved an arm and a leg against him and he responded by stretching toward her, and no feeling of wrongness or impropriety was introduced by this moment of something like tenderness, so they lay like that and breathed.

"You snore so loud," she said.

"I've been told that."

"I left you here and then went and worked on a paper and came back four hours later and you hadn't moved an inch. I let you sleep."

"Thanks."

There was a silence and Oscar took a moment to regard himself from the outside and noted how worried the current state of affairs would have made him even a week ago. But what was one more bad decision?

After another minute she said, "Out there on the road, did

you stop to think about the morality of this stuff? Coke, I mean. Facilitating its consumption specifically."

"I tried not to."

"It's something I've struggled with. But it's just coke. Who am I to deny the rich kids their coke?"

"That's not very universalizable, is it?"

"We're not in class."

"We're certainly not."

Oscar had tried cocaine exactly once, while visiting a friend as an undergrad. He had spent a few hours feeling like a once-in-a-generation genius, a capital-G Great Man destined to change the course of Western Thought, and had in fact left a party to sit on a bench under a streetlamp and scribble thoughts furiously in his little notebook. But when he went through his notes the next morning, he found them to be execrable where they were even coherent, and he became disgusted and ashamed with the psychotropic ruse that had been played on him, a feeling that lingered all day like the offensively weird taste in the back of his throat.

They were silent again and Oscar wondered if maybe he might as well just drift back to sleep but then she spoke again.

"Is it weird if I tell you I'm proud of you?"

"A little, yeah. I still feel pretty disgusting."

"Okay. I won't say it. Oh! I guess I owe you some money," she said.

"I get it just like that, huh?"

"I'm excited to give it to you."

"You're sweet."

"A man deserves the sweat of his brow."

Oscar sat up and leaned back against the headboard and rubbed his eyes.

Dawn said, "Although I must admit that I find it odd that you're still here."

"I can barely move," Oscar said, and it was true. He felt wrung out, his body come to collect the ruinous interest on all the adrenaline it had fronted him.

"Don't," she said. "I'll make breakfast."

They were sitting at her black marble kitchen island and eating perfectly cooked omelets and drinking coffee from a large French press when Ramos knocked once and entered through the front door, wearing all white from his sneakers to his baseball cap. He did a double take when he saw Oscar.

"Don't say anything," Dawn said to Ramos when she saw the way he looked at them together in their states of undress. "I mean, about this. You're allowed to speak."

Ramos walked over and placed his hands on the countertop. "So, nice job, I guess," he said to Oscar.

"Don't mention it," said Oscar.

"Is this it here?" Ramos said, gesturing at the bag.

"Open it," Dawn said.

Ramos hefted the bag onto the marble and unzipped it. He pursed his lips and nodded at the bricks within, a sign of respect. He raised a hand toward it and looked at Dawn as if to say, *may I?*

"Go ahead. It's killer."

Oscar hadn't seen her sample it. She must have done so when he was asleep.

Ramos wiggled his pinky finger into the hole that Oscar

had made with the key and extracted it with a pile the size of a large pea on his nail.

"Might want to go easy," Dawn said.

"Yeah?"

Dawn nodded.

He returned some of the pea to the bag and lifted half the original amount to his nose, covered one nostril with his free hand, and snorted.

"Well, hey," he said, eyes wide, looking at the corners of the room one after the other. "Hey hey hey. I'm getting the picture."

He regarded the satchel with new awe. "This'll straighten people out," he said.

"Not without your help, fair Ramos," Dawn said.

"Aye aye, capitán," Ramos said. He zipped up the satchel and slung it to his back. He gave Oscar a collegial shove in the shoulder. "Look at you, Mr. Drug Runner over here!" he said, and then left out the front door.

In fifteen seconds he came back inside. "What the fuck happened to the window?"

Oscar had the coffee mug halfway to his lips. "An unimaginably vast system of causality lashed out and passed through it," he said.

"It got shot," Dawn said. "Other parties became involved. Everything's fine. But be careful."

After he was gone, Oscar turned to Dawn. "Would you really have had him hurt me?"

"A girl shouldn't tell all of her secrets. Hey, speaking of that, stay right there. This is the fun part." Dawn dropped down off her kitchen stool and disappeared somewhere around the corner. In a minute she was back, carrying a manila envelope. She dropped it down in front of Oscar. "That's not all of it, obviously."

Oscar looked at the envelope and then blankly across the room.

"Well, come on," she said.

He picked up the envelope, pinched the sides so that the opening went ovoid, and looked down into it, keeping it at arm's length. An inch-thick wad of green lay at the bottom.

"That's five thousand dollars," Dawn said. "You ever seen that much in one place?"

Oscar took out the bills, held together with a rubber band. Compared to the briefcases of money that you see in movies, it was frankly unimpressive. But fifty one-hundred dollar bills was fifty one-hundred dollar bills. And more than that, they were *real*. And they were *his*. And no, he had never seen so much cash in one place.

He tried to feel exultant but couldn't quite muster it, which Dawn saw on his face.

"I know," she said. "We're good people—this doesn't feel very good at first. Try to think of the problems this can solve. Think of your family."

Something occurred to Oscar. "Where am I going to tell them I got this?" He was still staring into the envelope.

"Maybe you can say that you had another paper published."

"Ha!" Oscar laughed. "Hahaha!" But then he realized that Dawn wasn't kidding, and furthermore that she was right, that his family would believe whatever he told them.

"When do I get the rest?" he said.

"Very soon. First the cash must flow."

Oscar remembered something else. "Can I actually borrow your computer for a minute? I need to send an email."

He took her laptop back into her room, logged in to his email account, and opened a response to St. Germaine's last email.

Hi, Paul,

Your whole thing is basically just determinism, which is a term that you might want to ask your granddaughter to show you how to Google. There's been quite a lot written on the subject, and you'll you probably find some of it rather interesting. The matter of free will is not nearly as simple as you lead your "students" to believe—you're at least a few decades behind and I'd hate for you to embarrass yourself further. If you live in northern California, I'd even be happy to let you audit my class. Where do you live by the way? Your last email neglected to mention.

More importantly, there's one other issue that I wanted to touch upon, and that's that I'm given to understand that my father is under the impression that he owes you some type of monetary debt related to the bullshit you fed my mother. Surely we can agree, in recognition of how much you have already taken from my family, that this debt died with her?

Yours in compatibilism (which is another term you should look up),

Oscar

19

Oscar parted with Dawn and walked back to his apartment the long way, avoiding the heart of campus. Now that his mind was free to explore the implications of his actions, he didn't feel particularly great about supplying the student body with drugs that could, he considered now somehow for the first time, potentially kill them. The envelope full of cash was tucked into the front of his pants.

Walking was so slow. He missed the Range Rover already.

And God—how had he not thought of this, not even once, this was practically his job for God's sake—how much violence was represented by the mountain of coke for which he had just found a market? How much misery of an economically vulnerable people, deaths in crossfire, revenge killings, chainsaw beheadings?

He walked through the door of his apartment and fell into his bed without taking off his boots.

This was supposed to be a relief, a victory, to be back home safe with the whole thing over, but the one thing just led to more things and he still felt like shit and he still missed his mother and this wasn't really his home. And how much money was five thousand dollars, really? Even forty?

He pulled the covers over his body and then up over his head and tried to go to sleep even though it was only 4:00 p.m. and he wasn't tired. He clutched the envelope of money to his chest. *This impulse is bad,* he told himself, *you know what this is. This is like trying to die.* But the pull was too strong, and soon he was asleep, dreaming of lizards crawling up out of Roman ruins that were frozen in a sea of ice.

20

When he woke up early the next morning, his body yearned for its routine, and he let it take over. His Tuesday was not unlike most of his Tuesdays—he taught two classes, held his office hours, ate at the dining hall twice, and returned to his apartment in the evening to grade papers. He appreciated his life in a new light, the light that surrounded a man who had had a gun pointed at him, who had had a bullet slice the air very near his head.

He called his sister, intending to tell her that it turned out he might actually be able to help with some money and then get off the phone before she was able to collect herself enough to ask questions.

When she picked up, she assumed he was calling about their father. "I tried calling you like five times."

"Ah, shit, yes, I guess I assumed everything was okay, I'm sorry, I've been—"

"He showed up yesterday, but he won't tell me where he's

been. Didn't even have a story. Just said that he didn't want to talk about it and to please not press him."

"Well—yeah, that is weird."

"I never would have thought that Dad was capable of all this deceit."

"That's not deceit. Just secrecy. But I know what you mean."

"Well, whatever it is I don't like it."

"Me neither. But I think we just need to let him process in whatever way he can."

"All right, well, look, I've got to go. Kids need dinner."

They were off the phone before Oscar could mention the money. He would have to call back and try again tomorrow. He would call his father, as well.

For now, he had no idea what to do with the actual cash Dawn had given him. Was it safe to deposit it in his bank account? Until he had time to figure this out, he went to his room and put the envelope in his sock drawer. After a moment's thought, he took it back out and placed it instead in the lowest drawer, with his pants.

In the stillness of his apartment, his thoughts returned to St. Germaine. He had realized that rather than trying to forget about him, he wanted to find him. There was an image that his mind assembled and presented to him, although he kept pushing it away: Oscar standing, holding a wrench in some dusty Mexican landscape, while St. Germaine cowered in front of him, begging for mercy. But, he reminded himself, *I would never actually want to hurt him.* He only wanted to ask the man a few questions, questions that he couldn't recall at the moment but which would surely occur to him eventually.

When he sat down at his computer, he saw that he had another email from the department chair's administrative assistant, responding to the longer one that he had not yet brought himself to read:

Please confirm receipt of the below email. Thank you.

He was steeling himself to finally read it, when, as he looked at the screen, a new email popped up from St. Germaine. It read only:

Oscar, I can only reiterate how sorry I am for your loss. However, please do not contact me again.

Oscar immediately composed a long response, but when he read it back to himself, the words seemed like those of someone who was mentally unwell, which scared him. Instead, he deleted what he had written and copied in a link to purchase the free will anthology text that he taught in his class, and hit Send.

Afterward, he gathered what alcohol could still be found in the apartment and drank himself to sleep.

The next day, Oscar taught his two classes and then went to his office to hold his office hours as usual. He told himself that afterward, he would read the email from the department chair's assistant and then take the elevator to the chair's office and explain how he had had to miss a few more classes than he had expected in order to deal with his mother's death but that everything had now returned to normal and that he was looking forward to regaining focus on the work of teaching that he loved so much and that if perhaps a certain unsavory rumor had made its way to his attention, he would be more than happy to discuss its falsity.

His office hours were well attended, and he spent forty minutes going over a summary of Kant's aesthetics with a trio of energetic sophomores. After that, he met with a senior who wanted to inquire about a graduate school recommendation letter, which Oscar happily agreed to provide. On her way out, she held the door open for someone, and Ramos walked in.

A moment of dissonance pixilated Oscar's thoughts as a figure from his recent fever dream invaded his actual life in physical form, scratching his crotch, looking at Oscar's diplomas on the wall, the walking embodiment of bad news.

"It's crazy how they just let anyone walk around this campus, right?" Ramos said, sitting down in one of the two Windsor chairs in front of Oscar's desk. Instead of all white, today he wore all black—black jeans, black T-shirt, black sneakers, black baseball cap.

Oscar said the first thing that entered his mind. "What the hell are you doing here?"

"This may surprise you," Ramos said with a slow lilt to indicate that he wasn't answering the question, "but I never applied to college. I thought it was more prudent to enter the workforce."

"I feel compelled to ask you again—why are you here."

Something about the way Ramos slouched affectedly in his chair made it hard for Oscar to believe that he ever allowed himself to be intimidated by this kid. Now he was simply annoyed.

"Although, do you think it's too late for me to apply? I saw a flyer out there—how much does it cost per year here?"

"Do you reside in-state? Not that bad. Twelve K a year or something like that."

"State of intoxication. State of confusion. Oh by the way, I had the car window fixed. You owe me two hundred bucks."

"I am literally begging you to announce your purpose for being here."

"All right, shit, fine, man, I thought we were cool..." Ramos said, digging his phone out from his pocket. He thumbed opened an image. "One of my guys took this and sent it to me. You recognize?" He slid the phone across the desk.

Oscar looked at the image on the screen and a sheet of icy panic unfurled from his neck down to his fingertips.

It would be innocuous to anyone else, but how could he forget the grill of the black pickup truck, after he had watched it in his rearview chasing him across the desert?

"What is this? Where was it taken?" Oscar said, a rush of energy now warming a spot in his chest that the panic had frozen.

"I told you. One of my guys. Said he thought this truck was casing his shit two days in a row. Took this picture. Guy sped off." Ramos examined Oscar's face, which had gone white. "You look like you recognize."

"That's the truck. That was the guy. The fucking guy. Three guys. Were there three guys or just one guy?"

"My guy said it was just the one guy. What's his deal?"

"I think he was very disappointed that he didn't get to murder me." Oscar's hands were on his face.

"So what you're saying is we might actually be dealing with some shit here, then," said Ramos.

"Uh, yes. When was this taken?"

"This morning. You had words with this dude?"

"He's serious business, Ramos."

"You sayin' I ain't serious? I can handle my shit."

"How long have you even been doing this?"

"All I've *ever* been doing is this."

"I'll take that to mean, like, a year and a half."

"Stop playing, man. I came here for your opinion. How do you think we should proceed?"

Oscar looked up from his palms. "You've got to be kidding me."

He called Dawn as soon as Ramos left. "You're smart but you pick bad business partners."

"Ramos found you?"

"I need you to at least trick me into thinking that you understand the danger we are in."

There was a moment of silence on the other end of the line. "So you do think that's the guy? What'd you say his name was—Matadamas...?"

"It is him."

"Let's say it is. What do you think he wants?"

"You mean, besides the small mountain of cocaine? I think he thinks we have unfinished business or something. That we're connected. I don't know. It's weird."

"I'll be honest, some of these guys are real killers."

"If the things he told me were true, then I'd say that he definitely qualifies."

"This is not the kind of thing I ever really wanted to encounter."

"You're in the drug trade, Dawn."

"You are, too, if you hadn't noticed."

"Do you have the car?"

"Yeah."

"Where can you meet me?"

He had almost made it out of the room before he ran back to the desktop computer and clicked on the email from the chair's assistant before he could stop himself.

YOUR IMMEDIATE RESPONSE REQUESTED

As you will no doubt recall, last year's annual philosophy department barbecue was, although a fun afternoon overall, not without issue. A failure of some department members to RSVP in a timely manner meant that the insufficient number of hotdogs that had been purchased were quickly depleted, and a lack of clarity regarding who was contributing what resulted in the appearance of five containers of potato salad and none of macaroni salad...

It went on and on like this. Oscar grabbed his bag and sprinted out of the room.

She was waiting for him behind the wheel of the Range Rover in back of the department building.

"You don't have a license, right?" he said after getting in.

"Unfortunately I have to tell you that that was a lie."

They drove immediately off campus, hardly speaking. There were still some grains of shattered safety glass in the floor mat. Twenty minutes away, finally feeling somewhat safer, they pulled into a parking lot of a large sporting goods store.

"My money, it's just sitting in my drawer at home," he said. "Do you think it's safe?"

"I mean, no. It's probably the money that he wants, right? Why else would he follow you this far?" Dawn said. "He must know you wouldn't just hold on to the product."

"I have no idea," Oscar said. "Wait. That's not true. I think he wants to kill me."

Dawn's eyebrows furrowed, her mouth pursed. "That's such a weird thing to hear someone say."

"It's weird to say."

"Are you scared?"

"Yeah."

"Me, too."

"It's reasonable."

"I've got to be honest about something," Dawn said. "And I know it's extremely inconvenient and doesn't reflect well on me or my psyche, but I am suddenly turned on in a very strange way."

They shared a communicative look. Oscar thought, *I know less and less about this person.*

"Damn it," Oscar said and exhaled. Then they both took the same moment to confirm that it was sufficiently dark out and that there were no cars nearby and simultaneously unbuckled their seat belts. The car was spacious enough that when she climbed onto his lap, her legs folded with her ankles over his knees, her hair just barely brushed the roof. She kissed him with both hands on his neck, at the base of his jaw, as if she was trying to draw his face deeper into hers.

Belts, buttons, zippers.

"Oh my God," Oscar said, as her hand wrapped around him. She made a sound that meant the same thing.

Oscar tilted his neck a few degrees downward to gain some space to speak. "No, wait, I can't believe that I forgot, there's something I need to show you."

"Can it wait?" Dawn said.

Oscar leaned over, plunged his hand under the driver's side seat, and pulled out the nickel-plated .38. It was shinier than he remembered. In his hand it radiated malice, like it wanted to scream.

Dawn looked at it. A moment passed. "Are we going to die or what?"

"Eventually, yeah."

"That is some undergraduate bullshit," Dawn said and reached down next to the seat to find the lever that reclined the seat, and suddenly, with a jolt, like the slamming of a door, they were down.

One hour later they sat across from each other in a booth at a Denny's. Dawn ordered a double stack of pancakes and Oscar ordered a veggie burger. The gun was in the chest pocket of his jacket. Every few minutes, he touched it to make sure it was still there.

"You know about the gun laws in California?" Dawn said.

"They don't exactly smile on drug trafficking either."

"Have you ever fired a gun before?"

"I'm from Indiana."

"Oh, and that's like a war zone or something?"

"It's kind of just nowhere. But there are guns."

"You feel like you could point that thing at someone and shoot them?"

"Little ones like this are fairly inaccurate."

"That's not what I meant."

"I'm not going to shoot anybody," Oscar said.

"I think that to even consider that as a possibility might be overrating your ability at these kinds of things," Dawn said.

Oscar considered. She was probably right.

He ate two bites of his veggie burger and then signaled to the waitress and asked her for a cheeseburger.

"Coulda sworn you said veggie," the woman said.

"No, yeah, I did. Just a change of heart."

"Okay but are you gonna pay for both, because I'll get in trouble."

"I will."

The girl left.

Oscar still didn't have a plan but he had slowly come around to the idea of having a plan. The idea of getting cops involved, they agreed, was too fraught to even consider, especially given that the only crimes they had evidence of were their own. Which meant that, for now, there were really only two courses of action from which everything else would ramify: stay or go.

"What does that even mean, 'go'?" she said.

"Just for a few days."

"Like at a motel, I guess, or what?"

Oscar opened his mouth to ask her if she had any family

nearby she could stay with, but the words caught when he realized he probably should have asked her about this kind of stuff long ago. He didn't even know where she was from.

"Where are you from?" Oscar said.

"Las Vegas."

"I've never known anybody from Vegas."

"For most people it's not a place you're from but a place you end up in."

"Is that a song lyric?"

"Probably."

Oscar hesitated with what he was trying to say next, and Dawn said, "Now would probably be a good time to ask me about my family, while you're at it."

Oscar smiled a little, looked down. "What's the story with your family?"

Dawn slipped her feet out of her sandals and drew her legs up under her on the booth. She was small enough that she still fit under the table, even sitting on her ankles. "It's pretty dark, man."

"You don't have to tell me if you don't want to."

"No, it's okay. My dad killed my mom and then himself when I was seven."

Oscar had had his veggie burger halfway to his mouth to take a bite and now instead of eating it he was just holding it up, looking at it, some weird thing he had found in his hand.

"Jeez, ah, crap," Oscar said.

"Yeah, I know."

"That's so horrible."

"It made the news. You'll get a few hits when you Google it. He found her with another man and went basically insane with a shotgun. Shot the dog, even. I was at school at the time. I was lucky I wasn't close by, obviously."

"Dawn, I... I don't know how to react."

"It's okay. He was a piece of shit, if you can't guess. My mother, though, I loved. I can remember loving her. Her, I miss. I've never gotten anyone to tell me for sure, but I'm fairly certain she was a sex worker. She was twenty-three when she died."

"We don't have to keep talking about this."

There were very few other people in the place. At the counter, a burly man in a work jacket stirred sugar into his coffee, banging the spoon against the mug.

"Honestly, I don't mind it. It's keeping my mind off of things."

"I'm just trying to imagine what that would be like. What happens after something like that? Where did you go?"

"There were relatives but none the state deemed worthy of the honor. You do the foster home thing. You get moved around. I was kind of a bad kid but I kept my grades up and wrote one hell of a college admissions essay about overcoming adversity."

For the first time he had ever noticed, it looked like Dawn was trying to avoid his eye contact instead of the other way around.

"Do you have many memories of them? Your parents?"

Dawn folded up a corner of her napkin. Above and behind her, a fluorescent light that illuminated the menu above the counter flickered briefly, and then died forever.

"Whenever I think of my mom, I have this one memory— it's weird, the things that we remember. I'm sitting at this little kitchen table that we had, tucked into a nook under a bay window. We had one of those plastic kiddie pools set up outside, the kind where you just like dangle the garden hose for a while to fill it up, and I remember the way that the light reflected off the water onto the wall in front of me in the kitchen, dancing around. It was summer. The sun was up but it was dinnertime. I've got this plate of fish sticks in front of me, five or six of them in a neat little row, and I go for one of them and somehow it ends up on the floor. And I remember sitting there looking down at this fried brown fish stick lying on the white linoleum floor tile, which I can still see perfectly in my head, and thinking, this is very bad, we've got ourselves a real problem here, because that fish stick is down there and I'm all the way up here. I might have been in a high chair—is it possible to have memories of being in a high chair? Maybe I started to cry. And then my mom, who was talking on the phone— I remember that because she'd do this thing where she'd coil the cord around her whole arm, without stopping her conversation—she just comes over and leans down and picks the fish stick up and examines it for a second to make sure it didn't pick up anything from the floor and puts it back on my plate and goes back to whatever she was doing. And I remember I thought, well, that right there is my very own mom, and felt all kinds of warm emotions of positivity that I guess we don't have great words for."

Dawn crossed her arms over her chest, snuggled in against herself.

"That's a perfectly good memory," Oscar said.

"Sometimes I think, why couldn't I have held on to something more substantive? Like her comforting me after I hurt myself, tucking me into bed, or something like that. I try and try so hard to come up with something and I just keep coming back to that damn fish stick."

"I don't think I've had a fish stick in twenty-five years," Oscar said.

Dawn laughed.

"Do you think you'll meet her again someday?" Oscar said.

"My mother?"

Oscar nodded.

"That's a sideways way of asking me about God?"

"I suppose."

"You mean meet her in like a heaven type of deal?"

"Wherever."

"You've been thinking that about your own mom, huh?"

"Every day."

"I think about it. I think I'll see her again, yeah. Seems the less strange of the two options, honestly. Otherwise, what? She has a brutally hard, short, and unfair life and that's it? We never get to talk about it together, me and her, about what went wrong?" Dawn moved her napkin so that its edge was in line with the edge of the table. "I don't know. I don't think I'm doing a very good job of saying what I'm trying to say."

"I think I get it."

"I just really feel like there's got to be *something* going on here."

"I think so, too."

"Would you say that philosophy profs are a godless bunch, in general?"

"It varies. But yes."

"And what about yourself?"

"With me it's day-to-day."

"How about today?"

"Today I can barely believe what I've got in my pocket," Oscar said, and the girl came with the check.

They decided that it was too dangerous to go back and that they needed to stay away from campus while they figured out what to do. They drove twenty miles farther away and found a motel that had a room with a little kitchen area and a decent-sized bed. At the front desk Dawn turned her body away from the clerk and peeled off three twenties from a tightly rolled wad that she had in the duffel bag she had brought from her apartment. Oscar looked into the bag and saw more rolls of cash, and some clothes that looked like they might have been wrapped around something.

In the room, Oscar sat on the edge of the bed and laughed at what a connoisseur of these places he was becoming. This one seemed fairly nice.

Dawn sat down next to him on the bed. "I guess I owe you an apology about all this," she said.

"You know, at one point I thought you might be deliberately trying to ruin my life for fun."

"No. Never that. I promise I have always been pure of heart."

"You blackmailed me and threatened me with violence."

"Well, yeah, but—"

"I'm kidding, I know what you mean."

Dawn left to go across the street to a convenience store and buy necessities. After she was gone, Oscar felt strange and figured out after a moment that it was because he was apart from her. When she came back, carrying a plastic bag with a loaf of bread and jars of peanut butter and jelly, he was surprised by how quickly the feeling was relieved.

"You always keep expenses this low?" Oscar asked, gesturing toward the store-brand jelly that she took out of the bag and placed on the counter.

"I told you, I'm saving for grad school."

Oscar disrobed and climbed into the shower and turned the water as hot as he could handle. He positioned his face under the showerhead and stayed like that for a while, the scalding water pounding on his face and lidded eyeballs, which hurt a little.

The door to the bathroom opened. Dawn said, "I'm coming in," and a moment later she was in the shower with him, so quickly he didn't have time to object.

"Turn the heat down please," she said.

Her head came up to the height of his heart.

"There's not much room in here," Oscar said, uncomfortable.

Their voices echoed slightly in the small space and were affected by the water.

"Oh shut up," she said as she unwrapped the bar of soap. She saw that he was standing a few inches farther away from her than necessary and drew him to her by his hand. "You big baby," she said and rubbed his chest with soap.

He took her by the shoulders and turned them both around so she could get her hair wet. They washed each other, and then he held her for a while, and she draped one arm over his shoulder and the other around his back as if they were slow dancing but they weren't really moving at all. After a minute or two he felt her grip tighten and she began to sob, a few times, sharp and deep. He could feel her rib cage move jerkily against his. In another moment she was quiet again.

"You okay?" he said.

"Yeah."

Oscar thought he heard something from out in the room but then decided he hadn't. "We locked the door, right?" he said.

When he came out of the bathroom after brushing his teeth, Dawn was lying facedown on the bed with one towel around her body and another around her head. She had Oscar's laptop open in front of her.

"No password?" she said.

"Hey, come on," Oscar said, but didn't move to close it. Then he saw what she was watching: there was Paul St. Germaine, sitting in his chair, next to his plant, holding his dry-erase marker.

"This guy is a trip," she said.

"Please stop that," he said.

"Have you watched this whole thing? There's like—" she looked at the list of files "—twenty hours of video here."

"Not all of it. But it's all bullshit. Every word. Please—"

"Just let me watch for a minute."

"Dawn, that man is a demon. His allure cost my mother everything she had and she died under the spell of a lie. His goal is to separate the viewer as far from reality as possible. I hate him with my gut. My bones."

"From what I've heard of your mother, she doesn't sound overly credulous."

"Maybe not, but she was looking for some kind of something and he was more than happy to provide it."

"You don't think that maybe that might have been a good thing? Even if it was bullshit? If it made life easier for her?"

A change came over Oscar's face and his nostrils flared.

"Okay, okay, relax," she said.

"*Bullshit* a good thing?" he said, his voice wavering and rising. "It's supposed to be about truth. How is that not clear to you? Aren't you in my class? Truth is what I've dedicated my whole fucking life to. Ninety-nine percent of everything is bullshit and it takes a lifetime of hard work to find even just a tiny little fraction of that leftover one percent that means anything at all, and all I want to do is figure out one thing that's real before I die, and this guy is everything that stands in the way of that. He killed my mom with his lie, somehow, I'm sure of it, and when she died, she didn't even think that her life was hers."

"You say your 'whole fucking life' like you're not just twenty-nine."

"You don't believe me? You want to watch? Okay, let's watch."

He leaned over to hit Play just as Dawn drew her finger across the track pad and the cursor landed on top of the last file in the list. Session 15.

The sound came up, and then the production card, but there was no title. The letters of Samsara faded out and behind them Paul St. Germaine sat in his chair. The plant was

gone. The whiteboard was gone. He sat hunched over, elbows on his knees, fingers tented near his lips. He appeared
to be thinking. Nothing happened for fifteen seconds. Oscar
thought that maybe the image was frozen but he looked closer
and saw St. Germaine's shoulders move along with his breath
just slightly. Oscar thought he heard someone offscreen cough.
St. Germaine's eyes came up to meet the camera. He spoke.

"So. Our time together is almost over. I hope it's meant as
much to you as it has to me.

"There's not much left to cover. We've seen the problem,
and although it's a big one, we've seen how easy it is to overcome, when you're thinking clearly. And we've practiced some
exercises that we can do whenever we're feeling unsteady at
the wheel of our ship, exercises to remind us that there may
be a ship but there is in fact no wheel. And we've seen how
so many of our hurts come from fighting it, from damning
ourselves for that in which we had no part. So what could
be left for us to do?

"Let's just talk for a minute. Parting is hard, and I don't
want to say goodbye just yet."

His eyes glistened. He leaned forward.

"You're right to feel that life is bad. It's very bad. It's lonely
and painful and will end poorly no matter what. Every moment that we spend in comfort, not tearing each other to
shreds over the merest resource, is a miracle of human industry and ingenuity that has taken thousands of years to bring to
even this rough level of imperfection. This can be nice, these
baubles of civility and society that we've built for ourselves,
but at its core life is nothing more than a sick, distasteful joke
without a punchline. The only thing that's worse than life is

existence at all—so many endless light-years of emotionless universe, titanic swathes of violence both hot and cold bending through it in such scope that to truly fathom it would be to go insane. And think, in all that uncaring space, there is only one infinitesimally small location in which you might find something like what we would call love, and that's in your head, although it might feel like your heart, and no one will ever know about it except for you, and then you will die.

"But, I beg you!" St. Germaine held out his hands in front of him. "I've said this before and I'll repeat myself—there is no need for despair. You're on the carnival ride. Lift your hands with me, up off of the bar. We must not avert our eyes. Join me and look upon things as they are!"

He collected himself. Took a pause.

"What more beautiful truth could there be than 'nothing matters'? What could be more freeing?

"Maybe things didn't work out for you like you'd planned. Well, it doesn't matter. Maybe you've accomplished everything you've ever set out to do and are surrounded by material comfort and the love of your family. Well, that doesn't matter either. All are equal in the light of nothing matters. Maybe you've become one of those specters of ruin that the rest of us can scarcely even consider as real—well, the best piece of news is for you, and that is, that it doesn't matter.

"Maybe we'll all meet up in some heaven. In fact I hope we do! But it won't matter there either. It will go on and on and on not mattering. Crawl out of the cave and find yourself in another larger cave."

Dawn paused the video.

"This is a little upsetting," she said.

"I know."

"It's all like this?"

"Pretty much."

"I could see why this would piss you off."

"The man has perverted my field and swayed my mother under his perversion."

"I'm sorry. I think I get it now."

"Utter nonsense. And he took our money."

"I get it. I get it."

Dawn made them both peanut butter and jelly sandwiches and poured potato chips onto paper plates and they ate sitting next to each other on stools in the kitchenette. They did not speak but their knees remained in contact and occasionally they would reach out and lightly clutch each other's free hand.

Later they removed the comforter from the bed and lay down together, doing so in the absence of spontaneity for the first time. Somewhere, they had acquired an element of physical caution, stuck to them like burrs, and they approached each other carefully, as if they might burn their hands on each other's bodies. They coupled slowly at first and then faster than they ever had, calling out each other's names in dire whisper-yells, bedframe clanging. Afterward they lay together at odd angles breathing heavily, legs intertwined.

Some minutes later there was a flash of light at the edge of the curtains. Then another. Oscar put one hand on the floor so that he could reach the window from the bed and drew them back. Above the sodium lights by the parking lot and the line of road beyond, a silent lightning storm towered in the night sky, illuminating the hidden clouds in blinks and arcs, a roiling and layered vault of light, miles high. He lay back down with Dawn and they watched through the large window as it grew over the desert, coming toward them.

"I'll remember this moment for the rest of my life," Oscar said.

"Which one?"

"This one."

"What about this one?"

"This one, too. And this one. And this one."

Dawn smiled, which he didn't see because he was still looking out the window, and touched him in the small of his back.

They said nothing for a long time, watching, and then they were asleep.

Oscar's eyes opened. Dawn lay against him, asleep, her hand on his chest. It was still night. He shouldn't be awake. Something external had woken him up, but he didn't know what it was.

Then he heard a knock on the door and realized that it wasn't the first. He willed himself into believing that the knock had not existed and began to fall back asleep, but then it happened again. Three short, quick raps.

He sat up in bed, and Dawn's eyes opened and she started to say, "Wha—" but he covered her mouth with his hand.

"Probably just housekeeping," he mouthed to her, in the hopes that the words would make it true.

The gun was resting on top of the Gideon's Bible in the drawer next to the bed. He picked it up from the middle, around the cylinder, keeping his finger far away from the trigger.

As he crept slowly on the outsides of his feet toward the door, he felt entirely naked, and then remembered that he in fact was. He felt a draft on his ass.

He placed his free hand on the doorframe and leaned in to look through the peephole like a man extending his neck comfortably onto a chopping block.

In the external world, fish-eye distorted, stood Ramos.

"Motherfuck..." Oscar whispered.

Dawn looked at him from the bed inquisitively.

"It's Ramos," Oscar said. "Where are my pants?"

The first thing Oscar said to him when he opened the door was "how did you find this place?"

Ramos pointed to Dawn, who had quickly gotten dressed and sat in a chair by the window. "Hey, I know you're my boss or whatever but you can't just go and steal my car. And don't either of you ever look at your phones? I know you got nowhere to go. I been driving around all night to all the motels. Found it on my sixth try."

"I'd say it's maybe thirty percent your car," Dawn said.

"How did you know we were in this room?" Oscar said.

Ramos gestured toward the open blinds as if Oscar was an idiot.

"Well, you found us," Oscar said. "So what can we do for you?"

"Man, I just wanna know what's up. Nobody's answering their phones," he said, gesturing to Dawn. "If some hard-ass narcos are running around out there looking for us, I'm not trying to take that shit on by myself."

"It's the middle of the night. They're not looking for us, they're looking for me," Oscar said. "You've endangered yourself by coming here."

Ramos shrugged. "It's barely night. It's almost morning. Lemme sit down a minute. You got some water here?"

Oscar filled a plastic cup with water from the tap and handed it to Ramos. He drank it in one gulp and handed it back to Oscar as if to ask him to fill it again but Oscar tossed it in the trash bin.

"So what's the deal?" Ramos said.

Oscar was struck by the idea that there was something different about Ramos—his eyes a bit more sunken and dark-circled, maybe. His foot tapped. His hands remained plunged into his jean pockets.

Oscar had a thought, pushed the thought away, and then brought it back. At the toe of Ramos's white sneaker, there was something that could have been blood.

He looked at Ramos again, who was rubbing his forehead, covering his eyes.

"What's the matter with you?"

"What?"

"Are you okay?"

"Could I have some more water please?" As Oscar was looking at him, Ramos glanced once toward the door, then at him, then at Dawn. There was sweat on his face.

Oscar understood the truth but could not yet move, as if it might pass him over if he remained perfectly still.

"Oh, I've done something terrible," Ramos said. "I'm sorry. I had no choice."

Oscar raised the gun and almost pointed it at him and then lowered it. "Dawn!" he yelled even though she was quite nearby. "Get your shoes on!"

Dawn looked at each of them once and then dove for her sneakers, her gym bag.

Ramos had his hands out in front of him now.

"You son of a bitch," Oscar said, the cliché feeling absolutely perfect in his mouth.

"They found my daughter, man, I'm so sorry, what was I supposed to do?" Ramos began to cry.

Oscar clutched his head, took a step in one direction and then another back toward Ramos. "How much time do we have?" he said.

Ramos gestured toward the door as if to say such things were outside of his knowledge and control, such capricious forces could scarcely be guessed at.

Dawn was now at his side. Oscar looked in her eyes for a single instant and saw that she was with him, and then in one step he was at the door and through it and she was a half step behind and they were running, the gun in his right hand and her free hand in his left. They took a right down the outside corridor toward the flight of stairs that would take them down to the car, sixty yards away beyond a long row of chipped blue doors set in white stucco, Ramos yelling something behind them, and made it three long strides before a figure hove into view at the top of the stairs, first just one boot and then his legs and then framed perfectly in the rectangular space. Oscar knew it was Matadamas before he saw his face, and he

skidded to a stop with Dawn bumping into his back and he
raised the gun and fired.

Dawn screamed. Wherever the bullet went, it had no no-
ticeable effect. Matadamas ducked back behind the corner and
they turned around in the other direction, toward the only
other staircase at the opposite corner of the square-shaped
layout. Oscar knew without seeing that there would be another man coming up those stairs.

There was a small alcove sheltering some vending machines
and he pulled Dawn in behind him and moved through to
the exterior side and poked his head over the wall. Twenty
feet down to the pavement—too far to drop without risking
a broken leg.

"What are you doing?" Dawn said.

Against the side of the structure on the outside was a trellis covered in some type of creeping vine. It was flimsy, no
more than a quarter-inch thick of the type of wood used to
box oranges, but it was arranged in a diamond pattern that
might offer a toehold.

"Hurry," he said and threw a foot over the edge.

Her head was poking back around the corner, looking back
at where they came. "He's coming!" she said.

"Then fucking hurry!" Oscar said, now with the toe of
his boot wedged in one of the spaces of the trellis. He forgot
the gun on the ledge.

One step behind him, Dawn jammed the gun in her pocket
and vaulted over the ledge and landed with two feet in the
trellis. They began to scramble down.

They made it a quarter of the way before the trellis gave
out. Oscar felt it separate from the wall and bend outward

with sickening momentum, the opposite motion of a pole-vaulter's ascent. He had the odd sensation of quickly moving from vertical to horizontal, and while they fell he received a memory of Dawn throwing back the car seat in the parking lot the previous day.

They rode the collapse and toppled onto the asphalt below.

The earth punched Oscar in the shoulder and ribs and his wind rushed out of him as he rolled over. Dawn had also managed to roll and was already on her feet when Oscar stumbled up and then forward, his only thought to make it to the car, another fifty yards away.

The black pickup truck came around the corner with a surprising lack of speed, as if the man behind the wheel, who was not Matadamas, was looking for a parking spot. He did not yet see them although in another instant he would.

Dawn was one step ahead of Oscar, emerging out from the cover of a bush only a few feet from the driver's side door of the pickup.

Oscar watched her raise the gun and thought, *Oh no.*

But she didn't raise it far enough to shoot the man and instead leveled it to the top of the tire and fired. There was the report and then the slap of the tire blowing out. The driver raised his arms to his face and dove away over the gearshift. The truck continued to roll past them and they sprinted out behind it.

Oscar looked back when he was fifteen feet from their car, wrestling the keys out of the pocket of his jeans. The truck rolled into the side of the building fast enough to cave in the stucco of the lobby wall and shatter a pane of windows before coming to a stop. The rear side door opened and the man began to tumble out upside down, hands flailing for the asphalt.

Oscar grabbed the handle to the driver's side door. Matadamas came around a corner, a third man behind him, both with guns in their hands. The other man raised his and fired. Muzzle flash blossomed in the early morning dark.

A hole appeared in the rear driver's side door and then the front, and Oscar heard something mean and small burn the air over his head. He pulled open the door and jumped behind the wheel. Dawn was already in the passenger seat. He turned the key and the car came to life. Matadamas was thirty yards away, now running.

"Get us out of here!" Dawn screamed.

The car punched straight over the curb onto the grass. The engine roared, wheels grabbing nothing while the car bucked once through a decline in the turf and then biting in on the upslope on the other side, and then they were on road. He made one right and then one left, just gaining distance. They both panted for air. "Are you okay?" Oscar said.

"I've never fired a gun before."

"What did you think?"

"Loud."

"You could have shot that one guy."

"I don't really know if I was aiming at him or not." Dawn jumped in her seat. "Wait. What about Ramos? Turn the car around."

Oscar looked at her. "Dawn—he brought them to us."

"He's a coward. It's what I would have expected. You might have done the same. I won't leave him behind."

Oscar said, "Are you kidding me right now?"

"He's my partner. Yours, too, actually."

"You've already forgiven him for leading them to us. To kill us."

"No, I haven't. But that doesn't change things. I know you don't think so but he's a good man. That should matter. It matters to me."

Oscar knew that to abandon Ramos now was to guarantee his torture and death. Maybe, he thought, perhaps Ramos's blood would even satisfy Matadamas, lead him to call this whole thing off.

He saw safety ahead of him, the sign for the on-ramp to the highway half a mile away. If he could only turn off his moral sense like the flip of a switch, close down his receptors to Dawn's pleading, he could free himself from guilt and his body would do the rest, hit the on-ramp, get them the hell out of here. *What choice did I have?* he would say later.

"Please. Stop the car. For me. I know it's scary. I'm scared, too. But please, Oscar."

In his mind, Oscar saw St. Germaine lean forward in his chair and say, "You are not you." And Oscar saw that he was right. Oscar was not Oscar. Oscar was his cowardice, Oscar was his fear, Oscar was his desperate will to survive.

And yet, when he told his foot to apply pressure to brake, it did so, and the car slowed. He could barely believe it.

"Ah, Christ," he said.

"And let me drive," she said.

Oscar pulled over.

21

They'd made it less than a mile from the motel when they turned around. One hundred yards from the entrance to the parking lot, they waited at a red light. It seemed as if the fabric of society had not yet felt the ripples of what had transpired there moments before, despite the gunshots. No sirens could yet be heard. Theirs was the only car at the intersection.

From the passenger's seat, Oscar asked, "Dawn, what are we doing here?"

"We'll know in just a few seconds."

The light turned green and they advanced slowly toward the scene they had just fled. The breech in the collapsed motel office wall was empty, the truck gone. Two middle-aged men in shorts stood around the rubble of the wall, scratching their heads and pointing in various directions, but otherwise, there was nothing else that could be called a response to what had just happened here. Oscar could have convinced these men that they had been awoken by a bad dream, and that the crumbled wall was an odd coincidence.

"Look," Dawn said and pointed to a divot in the turf by the curb. The truck must have dug it with the rim of the wheel with the blown out-tire. The grass was chewed up in an arc that led away from them, down the road.

"Keep going," Oscar said.

A plastic chunk of the truck's fender lay on the curb. Beyond it, more small pieces. They were headed in the right direction.

"This is a bad idea," Oscar said.

"Is that an observation or an objection?"

He decided that since they still had a fully functional vehicle while the narcos probably didn't, they could try to observe from a safe distance and figure out what could be done once they had gathered whatever information they could gather.

"There's something I want to tell you," Oscar said.

"Okay."

"Back there, upstairs? I didn't mean to fire the gun. I just raised my hand toward him reflexively and it went off."

"Okay."

"I just feel like that's worth mentioning given that he didn't shoot at us fir—"

Dawn braked hard and pointed. "I bet they're over there."

"Let me hold the gun," Oscar said.

22

Once, years ago, there had been industry here, but it had taken its leave and its jobs with it and left its trappings behind. Dawn piloted the car onto the tarmac of an abandoned facility that looked like it might have once been involved in the production or transport of crude oil, a flat expanse of concrete dotted with tanks and storehouses and piles of rusty metal of unknown use.

"There!" she said.

The truck was parked in the lee of a warehouse some two hundred yards off, fully occluded from sight of the road. There was another vehicle as well, a smaller silver sedan, parked nearly nose-to-nose with the truck. Figures moved about.

"What do we do?" Oscar said.

"I thought I would know by now."

"Is Ramos there? Can you see?"

It was too far away to differentiate their faces, but it looked as if several of the figures were moving things from the damaged truck into the car. They were manhandling someone, moving him up against the wall by his wrists, which were behind his back. Oscar could tell by his bright white sneakers that it was Ramos. His pulse quickened.

"Get closer," Oscar said.

Dawn crept the vehicle forward. A large gas tank partially blocked them from view and she used it as cover as they approached. It was not yet obvious if they had been spotted, but soon they surely would be.

"Should we call the cops?" Dawn said.

Oscar opened the door and stepped out.

"What the hell are you doing?" she yelled at him. "Oscar! Get back in the car."

"Stay here," he said. "Leave it running."

There was a moment Oscar was sure, absolutely sure, that he was not in control of his actions—he had no other way to explain what he was currently doing—but then the feeling of agency returned, descending around his head like a halo. He looked at his hands and moved his fingers just to check, although he knew that was no proof.

He felt that he actually had a pretty good idea of what it would feel like to get shot, the brute impact, the oddness of the foreign body in his flesh like chewing on tinfoil, the shock, the delayed pain. *God, that would suck so much*, he thought. He was so scared and yet still moving. *Morality is not worth this*, he thought. *Turn back. Turn back now.*

He stepped out from behind the gas tank. He tucked the gun, which he calculated probably had two rounds left in the cylinder but now that he thought about it, too late to check, maybe had zero, in his waistband at the small of his back.

He approached the group with his empty hands at his sides. He was fifty, then forty yards away from the vehicles.

There were six humans: Matadamas, the two others that he recognized, two more that he did not, and Ramos, hands bound behind him, in the middle of the group, cowering at the base of the wall. One of the other men kicked him in the ribs.

What was my life, anyway? Oscar thought. There were periods in which he thought his life was quite good, and periods in which he felt perhaps even more strongly that it was quite bad, but the two never seemed very different from each other, and nothing ever happened to settle the issue one way or another. He was one of many billions and billions who had lived and died. Who was he to demand or expect that his life have meaning when the status had been awarded to so few, if any, before him?

In fleeting moments, he sometimes found himself imagining the lives, and particularly the deaths, of people whose existences had been entirely lost to human memory. The appeal of the exercise was in pairing the very realness of the fear and pain of these people with their complete insignificance, to imagine a feeling that was once so strong but that was now completely and utterly vanished, how real the person once felt to themselves compared to how unreal they now were. As he walked toward Matadamas and his men, several of these images reoccurred to him, bundled into one instant:

A Roman soldier feels his own ranks begin to crush in around him as the legion is surrounded at Cannae. He can hear the butchery that has begun at the flanks, but it will take four more hours before it reaches him. He cannot see over the helmets of the men next to him, but he can hear the cries of the centurions attempting to establish order over the panic. They are soon drowned out by screams. His last thoughts are of a small dog he had seen and played with, only twice, as a child in his village very far away.

Suddenly her first experience of light and cold, and such noise! People leaned over her, yelled at each other. This is no place to be at all, she thinks in a pure thought entirely unadorned with language, it's terrifying and loud, and what happened to that heartbeat? She dies quickly of a condition that her parents had been told might have been a risk.

Somewhere over the Rhine River Valley, a B-17 that contains ten human minds which in turn each contain absolute confidence that they will not survive this run takes a flak shell directly to the cockpit and plunges immediately straight down into a nosedive, the g-forces pinning each man in his position against the interior of the fuselage. As the screaming plane noses over, the small man in the ball turret has his field of vision reversed from the earth to the sky, and he watches the clouds as he falls from them, already in mourning for himself.

Near a cave in France, one of the first creatures who could be called human doubles over and clutches his stomach in agony. He knows nothing about the bad meat that he had eaten, nor do the figures crowded in concern around him; they know nothing about the world at all besides a few of its dangers. They huddle together at night and stare up into the stars without even the benefit of myth. The man knows only his pain, and when he dies he does not even have a name by which he can be remembered.

"Hey, fuckface!" Oscar shouted. Ramos was the first to see him. He looked up for an instant, his face bloodied and leaking, and they made eye contact. His upper lip curled in confusion, a flash of white teeth parting the rivulets of blood that ran from his nose. The man who had kicked him followed his gaze.

The man said something in Spanish and all the others turned to look at Oscar. Then they quickly shared a look among themselves, and then laughed, all of them except Matadamas.

Matadamas turned to face Oscar. He smiled and his hands shot up into the air in a V as if greeting an old friend.

"Oscar!" he called out. "I was just talking about you."

Oscar stopped moving toward the assemblage.

"You are a very interesting case, Oscar," Matadamas said, wagging his finger. "I think you might be crazy, even." He looked around to his men. "This is the fucking guy who fucking tried to shoot me! With my own gun! I have plenty by the way, Oscar." From inside his denim jacket he drew a much larger revolver than the one that Oscar had taken from him.

"Call me old-fashioned but I do prefer revolvers. It just seems like a more honest piece of machinery to me, the way you can see exactly how it works."

"What do you want?" Oscar said. By now he was used to it, this feeling of watching himself do things that he knew he couldn't actually be doing, saying things he would never say.

"Well, primarily the drugs, of course, yes? Or the money, if you've already moved it. Your friend has told me most of what I need to know. But your implication is correct—there is something more. Back when we first met? I've never had someone get one over on me like that. Total fluke. Really pissed me off, if we're being honest, and it left me thinking, how you were still out there somewhere, proud of how you had escaped me, and it angered me significantly. It felt like there was an imbalance that needed rectification. Not to put too fine a point on it, but I'm very much looking forward to killing you." He looked down at the massive revolver, then back up at Oscar, as if to say, *you get it*.

"I thought that might have been the case," Oscar said. "But you've got a business to run, and you'll want some kind of return on this investment of your time. I can probably get you the money. But I'd like you not to hurt this guy." He gestured to Ramos. "I don't think you're really very interested in him."

Ramos spat blood into the dust, fell back from his squatting position to sit in a heap against the wall.

Matadamas approached Ramos and extended the gleaming gun to his forehead like a blessing. Ramos closed his eyes and twitched. He made a small sound.

"This guy?" Matadamas said. "This guy right here? He's the one for whom you give a shit?"

Matadamas cocked the hammer back.

Oscar's heart, he was quite sure, stopped. After more than one instant of time perceivable to him, he realized that he was simply awaiting his next heartbeat as he regarded the image before him in complete stillness, two figures against a backdrop of brick, the man with the gun and the man on his knees both arranged in roughly triangular positions in ways that seemed almost intentionally composed, their physical relation to each other also arranged along similar aesthetic principles. Their faces, too, seemed to capture some kind of larger entirety, in the relation between the focused malevolence of one and abject terror in the other. A closed system. What he saw was beautiful, although that wasn't the right word.

Matadamas smiled again, said something in Spanish to the other men, and eased the hammer of the revolver gently back down with his thumb.

Wait, Oscar thought. Had Ramos just been executed and had his brain spared him the image of it for his sanity's sake, replacing it with what he was seeing now?

"I am rushing things," Matadamas said. He rubbed his eyes with thumb and forefinger, as if in frustration. "Oscar," Matadamas asked, "what I want to know is, how is it exactly that you think things work?"

"I know only that I have very little idea," Oscar said.

"Let me tell you about the world. That feeling you have, that you are the center of things? It means nothing, as you are about to see. It is completely illusory. This is not a story. You are not a character. I'm about to shoot your friend in the nose just to prove a point, the point that there is no point, and then I'm going to start chopping off your fingers until you tell me exactly what I want to know, and then I'm going to kill you as well, and that'll be the end of it, you understand? You won't even get to find out how it ends, because you'll be dead. You thought you could walk a straight line through chaos by walking it straight at me. Well, sorry, Charlie, no cigar."

None of the other men said a single word. Matadamas

strode three more paces toward Oscar. Oscar tried not to let his right hand, which hung at his side, move toward the gun at the back of his waistband.

"You are not a protagonist. I am. Do you know why? Because I'm blessed with the gift of violence, and if you go for that gun, you know as well as I that you'll never get it out of your pants. I am at home in these things. This is my air. You, I can see, are suffocating."

"Matadamas, I think you talk too much."

"You are funny, though, Oscar, I'll give you that."

Matadamas looked over Oscar's shoulder and saw Dawn in the car some forty yards off. He waved at her, fluttering his fingers up near his head. It seemed to Oscar that she had crept closer since he had gotten out.

Oscar said, "Here is what I propose." He awaited his own words. He opened his mouth again to speak.

Against the wall, Ramos sprang up, pushed his feet against the brick, and shoulder butted Matadamas in the small of his back. His revolver clattered to the ground, spun momentarily like a coin on a countertop. "Run!" he yelled.

Oscar stayed pinned to the spot. Either because to expose his back didn't seem like the right play or out of fear paralysis, he wouldn't have been able to say.

Ramos kicked at Matadamas, who easily sidestepped it, even as he was leaning over to pick up his gun, and Ramos fell backward on his ass.

As Oscar stood and watched, the narcos erupted in laughter, chuckling at first, then quickly building until they were clutching their stomachs, cackling, kicking at Ramos as he tried to regain his feet.

With the suddenness of a thunderclap, the wall a foot above their heads exploded into dust. The narcos hit the ground as Ramos scrambled to right himself. Oscar looked behind him—Dawn was standing on the running board leaning out from behind the driver's side door, a glinty object in her hand.

Matadamas raised his gun and this time the ground in front of him jumped up into shards. Oscar looked back again and saw that Dawn was reloading the rifle. Oscar began to move.

Ramos had scrambled, still not fully righted, a few steps closer to Oscar, and Oscar grabbed the zip tie that bound his hands behind his back and pulled him to his feet and the two men turned toward the car and ran.

The narcos were army-crawling into the lee of their car, except for Matadamas, who had advanced and dropped down to one knee and drew down on Dawn not slowly but with the practiced fluidity of someone who knows how to hit a target. Oscar punched him in the jaw and sent him sprawling.

A slice of air a few feet above his head was alive with bullets—Dawn was missing high to cover them.

When they made it to the car, Ramos dove across the back seat through the door that Dawn had opened. Oscar jumped behind the wheel as Dawn walked around in front of the hood, rifle still level, going to work on their cars now with a fresh magazine, putting a few rounds into the engine block of the truck and then blowing out two windows and one of the tires.

Dawn stood by the passenger door and fired until the gun clicked and then jumped in. Oscar turned the car around so sharply that he felt two of the wheels lift off the ground and had them pointed around back toward the road at the other end of the tarmac and floored it.

Oscar's ears rang with white noise loud as a scream. There was a conversation being held in the car, human voices, but nothing registered with him. It wasn't until the car was back on the road that his cognitive capacity returned to the point that he felt as if he could speak.

"What the hell was that?" he finally said.

"This is an M4 variant," Dawn said as she detached the stock from the receiver and stowed both components in her duffel.

"How long has that been there?"

"What the fuck?" Ramos said from the back seat, sitting up. He had brought his legs up and around the zip tie and now his bound hands lay in his lap.

"My possession of that," she pointed, "represents a sizable percentage of my entire illegal activity. And yes I was lying about never shooting a gun before. But that's my last lie."

Oscar started to say something, but a feeling of peace descended on him suddenly, and he returned his eyes to the road. Interesting—the road rose up higher and higher in his sight, blocking the horizon and then going past the top edge of the windshield in his field of vision until it looked as if he might be directing the car into a full vertical loop. Along with this new feeling came a sensation of warmth, of descending into some large fuzzy body of substance in a slow-motion belly flop.

"Oscar—" Dawn said, looking at him.

What? Oscar heard in his head but not in his ears.

His right hand came up holding a bit of the lower edge of the front of his shirt. He noticed that there was a hole in it.

He heard Dawn cry out.

Oscar saw the blood that had pooled in his lap and on the floor by the pedals.

This is a big problem, Oscar thought as the warmth moved over him. *Huge even, and I'm going to deal with it immediately just as soon as I wake up.* Then he nodded off backward as the car ran off the road.

23

When Oscar awoke he was in the passenger seat. The car was moving through a forest with trees so tall they blocked the sunlight and created a feeling of evening. Paul St. Germaine was driving.

"Paul?" Oscar said, and he turned his head toward him.

"Oscar!" he said. "Gosh—you need to understand that I'm so, so sorry about all this. This has all been a huge misunderstanding."

Oscar looked to the back seat. Ramos sat stock still in a rictus, eyes straight ahead, his hands on his knees.

Oscar looked back at Paul, who kept both hands on the wheel but directed his gaze at Oscar. His face was kind, his hair only slightly thinning.

"Is this real?" Oscar said.

"That depends on what you mean by real, of course," St. Germaine said, in his avuncular voice.

Oscar felt bathed in the most intense emotion. He brought

his hand to his face and found that tears were streaming down it. The road wound through the trees. He craned his neck to the base of the window to try to see the sky but found that he could not.

He turned around to look in the back seat. Ramos was gone. In his place sat Oscar's mother. She wore a knitted shawl over a red flannel, the same outfit she was wearing in a photo that had always stood on the mantel over the fireplace in their home.

"Oh, Mom, oh my God, Mom. Mom, I can't believe it's you."

His mother tilted her head and reached out to touch his shoulder and made a small look and sound that Oscar remembered as pure love.

"Bunny," she said, "My sweet baby boy. This was all such a bad idea!"

It felt as if all of Oscar's body was weeping, some essence of himself emanating from everywhere at once, hitting the air.

"I know, Mom. I don't know what I was thinking. I miss you so much. Why did you have to leave?"

"Oh, Oscar, I really, really didn't want to. But everything's going to be fine, bunny." She was sitting next to him now, cradling his head, speaking in a comforting whisper.

"What's happening to me, Mom?"

"You're dying, sweetheart. You got shot in the stomach. It's very bad."

"I'm so scared."

"It's okay to be scared. This is all very new and strange."

"So you're not real?"

"No, dear heart, I'm not real. But I still love you very, very much."

"It's so unfair."

"I know. I know."

"I don't think you're dying," St. Germaine said.

"He can be more optimistic than you'd think at first," she said.

Out the windshield Oscar could see the road beginning to darken, the wood becoming deeper and thicker as they proceeded, the branches moving in and down.

"There's supposed to be a white light," Oscar said.

"I know that that's something you hear about sometimes, bunny, but that can be explained via the function of panicking neurons."

"I know that. That's *my* thought. That's from my brain."

Oscar put his face in his hands, wiped away tears, but they continued in a torrent, wetting his cheeks entirely.

"You did this," he said to Paul. "You did all of this."

"We both know that's not true," he said and piloted the car to a stop.

"Bunny," his mother said, "this is as far as we can go. You've got to go on alone now."

"No! Please. I don't want to."

"Shh," his mother said. "It can't be so bad. Billions of people have done it. Your own mother has done it. Everybody's done it."

"Will I ever see you again?"

"I sure hope so," she said.

And then Oscar was alone, standing at the side of the road which was now a dirt path, leading deeper into the forest. He turned around to look back from where they had come, but blocking the path was a flat wall of a poorly textured low-resolution image of trees, something out of an old video game. He turned back around. There was no sound of anything other than the rustling of the vegetation. The wind began to rise, the branches bending under the gusts. He walked.

After a time, he saw that his father was walking alongside him.

"You know, you just missed Mom," Oscar said to him. "She was back there."

"I love that woman enormously," his father said. "When she died it just about took the life out of me."

They walked together side by side in silence.

"It's getting cold," his father said.

"I don't feel it," Oscar said.

"I'm concerned about that," his father said and pointed to Oscar's stomach. There was a large, clean, unbloody hole in his belly, a foot wide, like he was a doughnut. They could see right through to the other side.

"This is some kind of illusion," Oscar said. "Although it does hurt pretty bad."

His father shook his head. "Oscar, there's so much we wish we could tell you. Sadly, it's not allowed."

"Dad, I don't know what you're talking about."

"It's so sad," his father said and was gone.

Oscar continued. The path got more and more narrow and overgrown until he had to fight through low branches at the level of his face. Still, he felt the need to keep going.

Eventually he had to push through full vegetation, knifing into thick boughs with his hands to drive his body through the scratching branches, driven by an unknown purpose.

He did this for a long time—hours, days. At certain points,

he screamed, cried, wailed, was nearly overcome with frustration and despair, but continued on. Coming from everywhere, booming and full of echo, he listened to recitations of certain memories. Some were significant, but most were not—he heard his father give him the little speech that he gave when he handed over the keys to Oscar's first car, and then he heard an old classmate of his say something about the library's weekend hours, and he heard his own voice respond—was this an actual conversation he had had? He heard people that he understood to be his grandparents fighting bitterly over something trivial. He heard Dawn's voice over the sound of bowling pins: *Don't think. Decide.*

Then specific words fell away and people he had forgotten about for years spoke directly to him in tongues. He didn't understand their language but he received the basic point they were trying desperately to transmit—that this world is a veil and the veil is on fire.

Then, in an instant, he emerged into a clearing. It was bright—sun shone down through the cover in slanted columns and landed on fallen, moss-covered trees. The wind was still. From somewhere nearby he could hear some kind of babbling water—a pleasant little stream. In the middle of the clearing, emerging from the ground, was a pedestal of gleaming white marble with a Corinthian capital. A small object rested on top of it. He picked his way toward it through the scrub.

Sitting on the pedestal was a solitary fish stick.

Oscar knew without touching or smelling it that it was a fish stick and not a mozzarella stick or something similar. It seemed immensely powerful, radiating benevolence, just sitting there, four inches long, fried golden brown. The fish stick understood that you hurt, and it felt the same hurt. It was just as confused as you. It wanted the best for you. It wanted you to know that it was almost funny how awful this all was. It wept for you. It reached out for you.

Oscar reached out for it.

The fish stick said, "Oh shit."

24

"Oh shit, I think he's waking up."

"Bleeeeyahhh," Oscar said as he tried to sit up.

"Don't sit up," Dawn said.

It felt like gauze was drawn slowly away from Oscar's eyes. It was extremely unpleasant.

"What—what—" Oscar said.

Dawn put a hand on his forehead. "I know, I know, but relax."

Oscar looked around and found himself stretched out on an overstuffed couch in a narrow, sparse living room. For a moment he thought it was a train car.

Ramos was standing at the door of the trailer, calling to someone outside.

The overhead light hurt Oscar's eyes terribly. "Is there water?" he said. His mouth was so dry that it felt pointy at the edges, like it contained a mouth-sized pinecone.

Dawn told Ramos to get some water and in a moment a

glass was presented to him. Oscar raised his hand and watched it shake. Dawn, who was sitting in a folding plastic chair next to him, grabbed his arm to steady it.

He took a sip, Dawn took it away before he could have another, and he looked down at himself. His chest was bare, and his stomach was wrapped in a foot-wide band of clean white bandage. Running out of his arm was an IV line that connected to a bag of clear fluid that was duct-taped to the wall a few feet above him. On his legs were orange shorts that might have been swim trunks.

"We had to throw out your jeans, man," Ramos said. "Fucking nasty."

The screen door opened and a woman of about forty walked in, wiping her hands on a rag that she tucked into the back pocket of her cutoffs. "Are you in much pain?" she said. She had black curly hair tied in a knot behind her head.

"Please tell me where this is," Oscar said.

"Amani is a doctor," Dawn said.

"What your friend means is that I used to be a nurse."

"Not currently?"

"Not since my honorable discharge, honey. But I did two tours in Anbar Province. So I know gunshots."

"I got shot?" Oscar said.

"Yes," Dawn said.

"Wow," he said.

"Again," Amani said, "how much pain?"

Oscar tried to move his body and screamed and clutched himself. It hurt so bad he nearly passed back out. Dawn stroked his hair.

"Okay, yeah, no, that's expected," Amani said.

"How long was I gone?" Oscar said, breathing slowly now as he recovered from the pain.

"A long time," Dawn said. "All night."

"You won't remember, but you were in and out," Amani said.

"Couldn't have gone to a real hospital?" Oscar asked Dawn, adding, "No offense," to Amani.

"It was discussed," Dawn said.

"Amani was closer," Ramos said.

"It'll hurt like a bitch for a while but it could have been a lot worse," Amani said. "You're lucky. Went clean through and only nicked a few things."

Amani looked at everyone present in a moment of assessment and then snapped her fingers at Ramos and gestured toward the door. The two of them left.

After she was gone, Dawn said, "She literally used to babysit Ramos, how funny is that? Now she's like, a freelancer. I had her number in my phone."

Oscar tried to smile and then grimaced.

"How does it feel?" Dawn said.

"Like there's a pissed-off beehive under my lungs."

"I mean—to have been shot?"

Oscar was silent for a moment. "Was I that close to death?"

"Less from where it hit you than from where it could have hit you."

"It does give a certain funny feeling."

"It was extremely scary. I think I've retired from this."

"I was thinking the same thing."

"You have someone else's blood pumping in you now. Three bags."

★ ★ ★

They spent the day on Amani's property, which was a se-
cluded, charmingly scrubby patch of land on a small pond
up in a green protrusion of hills. Amani and Ramos washed
and worked on the car, which had taken some damage to the
front bumper and radiator when Oscar blacked out and ran
it into a tree, although most of the impact had been taken by
the expensive deer guard, which was now removed and cast
aside. Amani was confident she could fix it well enough with
a few parts she had lying around in the Quonset-style garage
structure behind the trailer, the same structure in which she
had worked on an anesthetized Oscar on the operating table
she kept under a blue tarp.

Dawn made them all egg and cheese sandwiches. (Oscar
was concerned about eating, but Amani assured him that the
bullet hadn't nicked his alimentary canal and that it would
be good for this strength.) After a few hours of moaning on
the couch, Oscar grew determined to stand up, and Dawn
helped him to his feet. A leaden center of pain swung down
through his middle and repositioned itself, but he found that
it didn't get much worse as he stood, and he allowed Dawn
to lead him by the elbow and shoulder as he haltingly stepped
across the floor and out through the screen door.

The sun felt good on his face. They spoke of nothing important while they strolled the grounds, no other houses or
structures in sight on the unfarmable land. She intermittently
asked him how he was feeling. At one point Ramos joined
them briefly to explain his actions, having the night before
already thrown himself on the ground at Dawn's feet to beg
for forgiveness.

He told Oscar about how Matadamas's men had pulled him off the street with a gun in his face and pulled a few of his toenails off, but it wasn't until they showed him cell phone pictures of his daughter's mother dropping her off at daycare that he had begged. Oscar thought he would feel more aggrieved by the betrayal but found that he couldn't blame him. What was he to this man, anyway, compared to his own daughter?

Oscar asked him if he had contacted the child's mother to tell her to get out of town with the child until things could be figured out and he said that he had. Ramos offered him his hand, not extended for a shake so much but just to make contact, and Oscar took it, absolving him. Why not? He would never have dealings with this man again.

Oscar asked Ramos what his real name was and he told him that it was Erwin.

Every half hour or so, one of them would check the news to see if there was any kind of report about what had happened yesterday. There was none.

Amani changed his bandages. While the old wrapping was removed, Oscar looked up at the ceiling—he would not look at the hole in himself.

"I know this sucks, honey," she said, "but we're gonna have to keep taking looks at this or it still could go south."

From a charger near the sink in the little kitchen, Oscar retrieved his cell phone, from which Dawn had done her best to wipe the blood, and limped slowly up the gravel road to the top of the hill where he could find some reception and call his father. He stood there in the sun and pleasant breeze with the phone to his ear. There was no answer.

While he stood there, three texts came in simultaneously from Sundeep. He registered only the words worried and missing class before he stopped reading.

Walking back down to the trailer, he stopped and lay down in a patch of grass and felt the waves of pain wash over him and tried to think of some evidence, and there was at least some, that the essence of existence was not suffering.

Some hours later, Oscar and Dawn sat in two Adirondack chairs that were positioned by the water. It appeared that some sort of pump fed the pond from the middle—there was a low bubble and gurgle. A few tiny orange fish darted in the murk.

"I don't suppose it would be possible to never leave this place," Oscar said.

"We can stay one night," Dawn said.

Dawn bathed herself in the outdoor shower. Oscar joined her at the edge of the spray of water, nude except for the bandages, and she scrubbed the exposed parts of him. Rivulets of dirt and dried blood ran down his legs. He bent over at the waist and she washed his hair.

That night Amani cooked burgers on a charcoal grill and the four of them sat around a small fire that Ramos made within a circle of stones, of which he was very proud. A bottle of whiskey was passed around. Oscar was allowed only one swig, so as not to thin his blood. Amani, with little prompting, told them her war stories with a surprising lack of reticence—mostly tales of grievous injury that seemed intended to highlight the extent to which the human body could be disassembled before it finally shut off for good.

The sun set fully. They brushed their teeth with their fingers.

Amani told them that the couch was a pullout but there was also a tent, and it would be a nice night for sleeping outside. Oscar and Dawn helped set up the tent in the yard. Amani gave them sleeping bags, said good-night, and went inside. After sniffing the couch and deciding that it needed some airing out after Oscar's night, Ramos lowered the back seats of the Range Rover and lay down across the trunk, windows open.

Oscar was still in tremendous pain. He and Dawn sat next to each other on the cinderblocks that served as the steps to the door of the trailer. The night was moonless. Above the trailer's roof, there was a line of hugely canopied trees, rustling in the rising wind, and then above that began the stars. Oscar imagined himself briefly in an ancient place, some type of fortified encampment, danger held just barely at bay, until the morning.

"I am oh so very tired," Oscar said.

Dawn took his arm and wrapped it around her shoulders. He sucked air over his teeth in pain. They listened to the grasshoppers.

"Is this over yet?" Oscar said.

"I'm not sure," Dawn said. "Does it feel over? Do you think those guys will still come back for you? Or us."

Oscar thought for a moment. "For some reason, it feels different than before. I think he might be done with me. I can't explain it. Also, at this point I think they're at least low on functional vehicles."

"For now."

They let this hang for a minute. Oscar broke the silence. "By the way—you really could have told me about the rifle."

"Oh yeah? What would that have changed?"

"Nothing, but—that's not the point. I should have known about it, that's all."

"That's exactly the point. Certain things, knowing them can kill you."

Dawn relaxed a degree, nestling her head deeper into the crook of his arm. He pressed his face against her hair and breathed in.

"How odd," she said, "that one thing just leads right to another and another. And then there you are."

"I know exactly what you mean," Oscar said.

They lay down together in the tent, in the pleasant smell of plastic and bug spray mingling with the smell of the fire that their clothes carried. In a few short moments he could tell that Dawn was asleep by her breathing—not snoring, only even and deep.

To calm himself and take his mind off the pain, Oscar imagined himself as his own ancestor, some man who had built boats, hewn keels and planks and masts from pliable trees and assembled them into vessels of warfare and trade.

Did such a man, in that line of work, also possess knowledge of the stars and how to set a course by them? Probably not. But in this vision, Ur-Oscar drags the boat he has made with his own hands out to the edge of the water. He is dressed in a resin-stained jerkin. It is nighttime, like now, and the stars are even brighter, not yet robbed by science of their mystery, and he launches himself into the dark chop by straining with an oar in the sand (physics here not accounted for—the long, deep-walled raiding boat of Oscar's imagination certainly too large to be dragged or launched by one man).

Oscar tried to see through Ur-Oscar's eyes as he lies down on his back in the night in the boat he built and looks up at the stars as they yaw in his vision framed by the sides of the hull, adrift in a current that he chooses not to let concern him, and falls asleep.

25

Oscar awoke in an instant, before dawn, and found himself under a pall of dread, the interior of his sleeping bag slick with sweat. He fished his phone out of the little pocket of his swim trunks—no reception, but it still had a charge. Quietly, without waking Dawn, he extracted himself from the sleeping bag and stood up. The pain was somewhat less than yesterday or at least dulled by familiarity. He stepped out of the tent and began to walk up the hill in the lightening dark to where he had found reception the day before.

As he walked he felt more than ever that he was not in control—this was the script and he was an actor, or not an actor but an audience member, his body merely a prop.

When he crested the hill, he looked around at the other nearby hills furled in tall grasses, blue in the dark, their motion in the breeze slowed by dew. There was very little sound here.

He took out his phone and looked at it. Somehow, he knew it would ring, and then it did.

Something terrible became known to him. Oscar under-stood that he was having one of those moments, he figured you might only get one in each epoch of your life, where the massive clockwork that ticks just outside the boundaries of perception in order to maintain the motion of reality is re-vealed for a single instant, and something totally inexplicable and impossible becomes perfectly, obviously clear.

Some berm that had been holding on within him twisted against itself and shattered.

He answered the phone.

"Hi, Gracie."

"Oh my God, Oscar, thank God you picked up. I don't know what to do."

"Calm down and tell me what's happened."

"I found something at Dad's. A note—a letter. He wasn't picking up his phone so I came over here and the door was locked, you know they never locked the door, I had to go back and look for my key, I forgot I even had one—"

"And there was a note," Oscar said.

"It's a few pages long. It was sitting right here on the kitchen table, addressed to you and me. Handwritten. God, I'm really scared."

"Can you read it to me please?"

In a frantic voice, short of breath, Grace began:

To my dear children,

First of all, I want you to know that I tried my best, like I've always done, like your mother and I taught the two of you to do. You should know that I had always kind of counted on me going first (most men do), and it turned out I was just totally un-

prepared to be without her. That sounds selfish, and I guess it is, but I couldn't believe how blindsided I was. Even still, sitting here writing this, it doesn't feel real.

What I'm trying to say is, life is different once the light has gone out of it. This is something that I'll never be able to explain with words and I hope you'll never know it, because feeling it is the only way to know it. And I know you might say, give it some time and things will improve, and I would respond that I am quite certain that that's not true.

And the fact that she was taken from me—it just drove me nuts. Sitting here in this empty house thinking about how I failed to save her, how she spent the last of our time together seeking out help from another man.

I know he isn't responsible, not really, for her death—it was such a freak, random thing—but also, in another sense, not the kind of sense that holds up in court, I know that he was. Again, it's hard for me to explain.

There is more to say—so much, that it's pointless to try.

I'm sorry, more than anything else.

Anyway. That's it, I guess. I keep trying to find a good ending so instead I'll just end it here. You know I've never been much of a writer, like your mother was.

Christ, this looks like a suicide note! I don't intend to die. But if you haven't heard about something happening and you find this note, please direct the police to the following address:

"And then there's an address in New Mexico," Gracie finished. "Oscar, what the hell is in New Mexico?"

Oscar knew.

"Grace, I need you to do one more thing," Oscar said. "The closet in the kitchen with the .308..."

"I'm in the kitchen right now," she said.

There was a rustling on the line.

"It's gone! Jesus, Oscar, it's not here! What is going on? Should we call the police?"

"No, don't do that. That address—please read it to me slowly."

She did.

"And when was the last time you saw him?" Oscar asked.

"Yesterday morning."

"Okay. Stay calm. Don't do anything until you hear from me."

He made her promise and then said goodbye.

As he ended the call he heard gravel crunch, and he turned around and saw that Dawn had followed him.

"You should be resting," she said.

Her face became worried when she looked into his eyes.

"Who were you just talking to?"

A wave of pain rolled out from Oscar's wound and he crumbled to his knees and sat down on the ground.

She called out his name and sat by his side.

"It's all real," Oscar said.

"What? I don't understand," Dawn said. She had one hand on his hip, the other held his cheek so she could look into his eyes.

"All disasters are inevitable. Now or later, what's the difference?"

"Oscar...you're scaring me." She began to cry. "Who was that? Your family? Let me see the phone."

Oscar kept it away from her. He could barely believe how much sorrow and anger could exist inside himself at the same time. "Reality has come up alongside my life."

He looked into her eyes. "We really came close to pulling this off. Can you think of a world where we might have ended up together?"

She put a hand to his forehead. "Jesus, you're burning up. We need to change your bandage. Stay right here, okay? Please."

Dawn ran down the hill in the direction of the Quonset hut.

After another moment, Oscar stood up. He watched her moving away, slipping in the gravel, and felt a fathomless sympathy for her, and a sadness that he would never truly know her, just as he would never truly know anyone.

When she was out of sight, he went down the hill from another angle and approached the trailer from the rear. From a laundry line outside, he pulled a too-small bathrobe and donned it over his bare chest. Inside, he found a notebook and a pen and the keys to the car. Amani appeared to be gone.

He felt himself to be gliding from place to place, lighter, either totally depleted or totally purified.

Back outside, he got in the driver's seat and jotted down the address Grace had read to him, although he would not have been capable of forgetting it. He keyed it into the GPS and examined the route. It would take all day, but to Oscar it felt as if he was unbelievably, miraculously near, and had been all this time. Then he tested out the route with his father's address as the point of origin—twice as long, but he had had up to a full day's head start. It would be close.

He remembered that Ramos was in the trunk when he heard him stir.

"Time to wake up," Oscar said.

Ramos's head popped up over the partition, rubbing his eyes. "What time is it?"

Oscar jumped out of the driver's seat, went around back to pop open the trunk, and pulled Ramos out by his ankles.

"The fuck?" Ramos said as he spilled into the dirt and tried to right himself.

Dawn appeared right as Oscar got back behind the wheel and shut the door. "Where the hell are you going?" She dropped the bandages she was carrying and pulled on the handle to the door but Oscar had locked it.

He lowered the window enough that she could hear his voice. "Please," he said, "I need to go. I think I can still save him."

"Save who?"

"You'll be safer this way. I only fuck things up," he said, not looking at her. "Amani can drive you back in her car."

Their faces were six inches apart. Dawn had both of her palms on the glass. "What are you doing? You can't just leave me!"

Oscar started the car. "I have to. I'm sorry."

Dawn had fresh tears in her eyes. "Whatever you're thinking about doing—you have a choice. I promise."

This he did not even consider. "You don't understand," he said.

"Oscar, please," Dawn said. Her voice cracked. "Please

don't leave me. Let's go home. Please don't leave me." But the car was already moving.

She ran after Oscar as he pulled out, begging him to stop, until the car picked up enough speed to separate, and then she dropped to her knees in the dust kicked up by the tires. Oscar watched in his rearview mirror for a moment too long, and almost ran into a tree before he righted the wheel.

On the road out of the property, he saw Amani returning from a sunrise jog and slowed next to her and lowered the window. She was sweaty and confused to see only him in the car. He took all of the bills from his wallet, which he noticed were stained and damp with blood, and passed them to her.

"I'm sorry, thank you for saving my life. I've got to take this bathrobe."

26

He drove in silence, hardly noticing his surroundings, consumed with hate, hunched over his burning wounds. His phone chimed with incoming calls and texts but he didn't look to see who they were from before he allowed the battery to die. Sometime in the early afternoon, standing at a gas pump in his bloody boots, bathrobe and swim trunks, he saw an advertisement for the Nevada state lottery and realized he had crossed state lines.

He stood there, baking in the heat of the tarmac, holding the pump in his right hand, his left clutched over his stomach, and made eye contact with a man in a Prius who looked at him with amusement or confusion. He cinched the robe tighter to cover the bandages.

Out into a new desert. Towering red and orange rock formations rose up on either side of the road. Oscar was aware that they were beautiful but he could not stop thinking about what was soon to happen. His pain increased. Slowly, in his suffering, it seemed to Oscar as if the true state of things was being shown to him, a door that had always been closed to him now unlocked, everything as bad as he had always feared and yet nothing to fear.

His mother's life, his father's—they had come and gone. They had done their best with what they had been given and tried to love as best they could and for a time, a long time even, that had been enough, but in the end there was no escape. And now Oscar's life, as well. He felt almost honored, clothed in something like immortality, to be the bearer of such a great secret.

He turned off the AC, opened the windows. The car's dashboard told him that it was 103 degrees outside. The heat rushed in and he began to sweat. As he drove, he recalled images from the past—his father teaching him how to ride a bicycle in the parking lot of the high school, his mother helping him move into his freshman dorm. Things like this. More than once he was sure that he had just been asleep the moment before, but his hands were steady and kept the car on the road. Eventually he began to hallucinate.

The edges of the road dripped laterally into the desert, which pulsed and undulated in the heat. For a moment, he saw a figure sitting on the hood of the car. He drove over a soda can in the road, and he heard it scream in pain, a piercing, awful sound that reverberated in his head, and he screamed along with it. The sun set.

27

Just after 9:00 p.m., he coasted out of the desert into a small, moneyed residential community that sprang up suddenly like a natural outcropping of precious ore. He wove the gracefully curled streets and regarded the three-story houses with tasteful statuary and perfect green lawns in defiance of the climate. The GPS informed him that he was one hundred yards from his destination.

He parked on the other side of the street, a few houses down. The house he was looking at was pleasant and still. Lights were on in the first-floor windows, through which Oscar could see a chandelier and the corner of a bookcase.

Parked in front of the house, right at the curb just as if it belonged there, was his father's car.

Oscar sat there for thirty minutes, frozen in place, terrified. Voices spoke to him, which he knew weren't real, in a string of curses and slurs.

Finally he found himself to be moving. He slowly opened

the door and stepped down into the darkness. The heat of the day was still held in the ground.

He looked down at fresh blood seeping through his bandages and frowned. He stared at the blooming spots and willed them to go away and, as he watched, they did exactly that, shrinking until they disappeared. *That's better*, he thought. He had not eaten or drank all day.

The house had no wall or gate. He walked across the front yard on a stone path that led between the house and garage, around back through an arch trellis near the kitchen window, past the humming central air unit to the backyard, saw a sliding glass patio door, felt that it was unlocked, slid it open, and stepped inside.

The air conditioning felt amazing on his face. He sensed a stir of life coming from deeper within the house.

There was still the chance for him to turn around and leave, to call the police. A small voice, Dawn's voice, told him that that would be the smart thing to do.

But he had come all this way.

Four more steps and he was standing in the halogen light of the kitchen face-to-face with an older man who exclaimed, "Sweet lord Jesus," and dropped a glass of water onto the linoleum floor and recoiled against the wall as the glass shattered. The man was in fact Oscar's father. He made a kind of croaking sound.

"Oscar—it's you."

Oscar saw the old .308 propped up against the gleaming stovetop.

"Oh, I've done something terrible," Lee said.

Temporarily, Oscar could not speak.

Lee walked around to the living room and Oscar followed. Plush furniture was arranged around hardwood tables. Landscapes and still lifes hung on the wall.

In the middle of the room, on a huge bearskin rug, a white-haired man in plaid pajamas was duct-taped to a kitchen chair. He had a dish towel in his mouth, also duct-taped. His eyes, wet with terror, darted between the two of them.

"Dad—is this...?"

"Yes, of course. Where are your clothes? You're bleeding."

"What were you planning on doing?"

Lee ran a hand through his hair and looked around. He had the expression of a man who had just woken up to discover the bed he was lying in was on fire. "I... I just wanted to talk to him. I don't think I was ever really going to hurt him."

The man with the towel in his mouth made a muffled sound.

"How did you find this place?" Oscar said. The edges of this scene were drawing in on him a bit and he had to push them back into place.

"I found the address in a notebook of your mother's. I don't know how or why she had it. That was one of the things I wanted to ask him. I only just got here a little while ago. We shouldn't stay."

Oscar looked around, bewildered. There were framed photos on the mantel, a large grandfather clock at the foot of the stairs. He looked at the man in the chair again, who seemed to shake somewhat.

"Dad—what have you done?" Oscar had heard the phrase a million times but never used it.

"I haven't done anything," Lee said. "Not really."

"Well!" Oscar said, holding his palms up in disbelief. "What happened?"

"What's happened to you?" Lee said, pointing toward the bandages.

"I need this whole thing to slow down," Oscar said and went and sat on the couch facing the man in the chair. When he sat, he felt something heavy move in the pocket of the robe and he reached in to find Matadamas's revolver. *Hmm.* He didn't remember that.

"He wasn't making any sense," Lee said. "So I had to do this. I only hit him a single time."

"You haven't spoken at all?"

"Not properly."

Lee came over and sat next to him on the couch. They both stopped and looked at the man in the chair.

Oscar put his hand on the tape that covered the man's mouth.

"Hi, we're the Boatwrights," he said. "You must be Paul St. Germaine. Please don't scream."

He ripped off the tape.

Paul spat out the towel and gasped for air. "Please," he said. "I can't feel my feet."

"Delia Boatwright," Oscar said. "Do you really remember her or were you lying?"

"What? Delia..." St. Germaine said, eyes blank. "I'm trying..."

"She believed in you," Lee said.

"I've watched your tapes," Oscar said.

"Ah...yes, Delia, of course. But please, my feet..."

Lee got down on one knee and loosened the tape around

Paul's ankles. Relief washed over his face. He took a breath. "Delia—a very smart woman. Please, whatever you want, you can have it. I'll take you around. There's much of value."

This man was almost completely unrecognizable from the person Oscar had seen on his laptop screen. He was frail and diminished, the effects of his age no longer dignifying.

"My father had come here to kill you. I've considered stopping him."

"I'm embarrassed to say that he's right," Lee said and stood up and turned away as a way of hiding his face. "I'm sorry for striking you earlier."

St. Germaine looked Oscar up and down. "Young man, I don't know what happened to you but you appear to be bleeding. Let me get you some bandages."

Lee had moved to the mantel and picked up a framed black-and-white photograph of a couple on their wedding day in what looked like the early '50s.

"Where is your wife?" Lee said.

"To my great sadness, Samantha died seven years and, let's see, eight months ago."

"My Delia died just recently."

"Your son had informed me. I'm very sorry for your loss," St. Germaine said. "There's nothing harder."

"Yes."

"She was wonderful. Kind and funny."

"Don't talk about her," Lee said.

"And this is why you've come here to kill me?" St. Germaine said.

"Something like that."

"You consider me responsible."

"I know that it's not exactly fair," Lee said.

St. Germaine craned his neck to look around, exhaled. His hands were bound at his side but he made a thoughtful gesture with his mouth, a pursing of the lips in consideration.

"Well, I'm—let's see, how old?—I just turned eighty-four. That's more time than most get, and it's been a better life than I've deserved. My body is completing its failure regardless. That rifle, though—it's a large caliber? I'll admit that I'm afraid of pain."

"I'm no longer sure about it at all," Lee said.

"Forget about that for a minute," Oscar said. "Everyone shut up for just one minute."

They did. In the silence, the grandfather clock ticked. In a flash, Oscar understood now—*oh, right, I've died. I was shot in the stomach and I died, which makes perfect sense, and all of this is something else entirely. So I might as well proceed.*

"I want to ask you some questions," Oscar said and then experienced a wave of physical pain so intense that he almost fell forward onto the floor. He shook his head to try to clear it.

"I want to ask you," Oscar said after he regained himself, "I want to look on your face and ask you—you do believe what you say?"

Lee said, "I think I need to step away. I feel absolutely terrible about this," and left the room.

"I believe every word of every idea to which I've ever attached my name," St. Germaine said.

"There is no idea. It's nihilism. Ignorance."

"Oscar," St. Germaine said, "I'm worried that perhaps you've missed the point. Say, would you like some food?"

For an instant, Oscar thought he saw a face in the lines of the drapes and almost screamed, but then it was gone.

Oscar continued, "Wait—what I'm trying to say is—are you a good man? Do you think you're a good man? Is that even something one should be concerned with being?"

Something like a smile crossed St. Germaine's face. "I hope—I believe—that the people who encounter my work and connect with it often have their lives improved in a way that I think you would probably want to call 'good.'"

"My mother—you cheated her. You sold her a lie. She died in ignorance and in debt to you."

Paul snapped his head and restrained torso toward Oscar. The chair budged half an inch. "When Delia came to me, she was in constant misery. She still sought the love of God and could not bear the lack of it. She spoke of killing herself—I'm sorry if this news is a surprise to you. I freed her from that."

"Well, you fucking overcharged. And your bullshit is not the love of God."

"I never want anyone to spend more than they can afford. And furthermore, what was my lie?" St. Germaine asked of Oscar.

"That this life is escapable."

St. Germaine smiled. "I wish we had met under more pleasant circumstances, Oscar. I feel as if we would have gotten on quite well. Of course life is escapable. What could be easier?"

"You misunderstand me," Oscar said.

They sat apart from each other in silence for ten seconds. St. Germaine's eyes lit up. "You know," he said, "of course. That's right. I remember you now."

Oscar looked up.

"Delia mentioned you in our first interview in Hawaii. She was scared that the thing that plagued her lived on in you, as well."

The grandfather clock struck the hour and began to chime. Oscar clutched his stomach.

"You should know that she loved you very much. In fact, her worry over you was hurting her. I taught her that your life was beyond her control, just as her own life was. To release her from this weight, I had to convince her to sever the connection she felt with you."

As Oscar took a breath and opened his mouth to speak, a rifle report cracked from somewhere behind the house. The echo was lost over the desert.

Oscar bolted up. The room tilted and then righted. He dug the pistol out of his pocket and aimed it at St. Germaine.

"It's okay," St. Germaine said.

The gun shook in Oscar's hands. He didn't want to go see what had happened outside. Oscar lowered the gun and moved down the short hallway to where he could see the patio door, standing fully ajar, a rectangle of blackness filled with night. He took one step toward it and stopped. All was still.

"Please," St. Germaine said from behind him, "sit."

Oscar went back to where he was sitting previously and cradled his head in his hands, still holding the gun.

"There's nothing you could have done," St. Germaine said.

"That's not true," Oscar moaned. "That's just not true."

"Shhh," St. Germaine said. "It doesn't have to hurt like this."

Oscar stood up, walked over to the chair, and placed the muzzle of the gun between St. Germaine's eyes, which the man had tilted up to him, and breathed deeply before speaking. "Whether or not I'm going to pull this trigger—that's already been determined?" He knew this was an overly simple way to state it.

Paul closed his eyes and smiled like a man hearing a beloved piece of music from a passing car. "Either way, as you see," he said, "it's out of my hands."

To his great shock and disgust, Oscar felt his finger pull the trigger.

The gun clicked.

"Oh my God," he said.

"Hah!" St. Germaine exclaimed.

From some distance that didn't seem very far away, they heard the sound of sirens.

"I think it would be best if you stayed put," St. Germaine said. "They'll be able to get you patched up."

Suddenly, Oscar could sense a vague outline of the full foolishness of what he had done. In a thrall of panic, he knocked the kitchen chair with Paul in it on its side. The air left St. Germaine when he hit the carpet.

Oscar lurched toward the patio door. The hallway seemed as if it had repositioned itself diagonally, on its corner, and he kept one arm on the wall to counteract this rotation. Behind him, Paul flopped around on the floor trying to right himself.

At the threshold of the door, Oscar stopped, terrified about what he'd find on the other side.

But when he stepped through into the air, with a feeling like falling, there was nothing of note on the other side. Just a large outdoor table under a trellis, surrounded by empty chairs.

"Dad?" he said quietly, and then again, more loudly. "Dad?" The sirens were closer now.

He felt around in the pockets of the robe for the keys to the car and found nothing.

Although to leave out the front of Paul's house would have meant to step into the suburbs, leaving out the back was stepping directly into the desert. Oscar scrabbled over some tastefully arranged stones and a chaise lounge and then a larger boulder that marked the end of the property and looked out to find sheer nothingness. Pure, flat night, with nothing on the horizon and no moon to light the way. His father must be out there.

He looked back at the house, which was now several hundred yards in the distance, although that couldn't be right, he couldn't have covered that much ground already. He thought he could make out someone standing in the rectangle of light that was the open sliding door, yelling something.

Oscar walked deeper into the night. It was cold now, and he pulled the bloody robe tighter. The next time he turned around, he realized the ground had sloped downward and he could no longer see the house at all.

He had expected that his pain would eventually begin to subside but it was getting worse and spreading. He moaned like an animal. Bile rose in his throat.

An unencumbered wind was rising, and as he stumbled over the hard ground he realized fully how bad this was. Fear spiked inside him. And then it fell away.

He wondered, if he had had another chance, how far back in time he would have had to go for things to turn out okay in the end. Long before he met Dawn, that was obvious. Back before he chose a profession. Maybe if he could go far enough back to significantly alter the life of his mother, maybe to her childhood, where he could try to stop the world from inflicting itself on her the way it had—that would probably be simpler than trying to change whatever it was within her that made her feel life's offenses so keenly.

He lay down for a minute in the rocky dust, curled up, closed his eyes, and tried to make it so. He figured it was worth a try—it seemed like such a simple impediment to overcome: merely time and space. Why be here, now, when he could just as easily be there, then? But nothing happened. He was still, somehow, tethered to this place, maddened by the boundaries of his perception.

When he stood up again, it was freezing. He began to shiver.

Could he turn back? He realized he didn't know which way back was and couldn't see his tracks.

Eventually, if he tried to stay pointed downhill where he could sense an incline, he would hit a stream or a river, and if he went far enough in one direction along it, it seemed to follow, he would eventually hit a road.

Forms suggested themselves to him in the dark; he thought perhaps scrub bushes or cacti, but when he got close they dissolved and he walked right clean through the space where he thought they had been, his hands out in front of him like a sleepwalker.

His feet blistered, his pace slowed. Not knowing what to do, he sat down on the ground to think this through. He tried to warm himself with thoughts of love and kindness. He called out to his father and then to God.

Just then, in the space of one second, the cloudbank that was covering the moon rolled away, and the light that fell down like gray gauze was startlingly bright compared to what had preceded it.

The light allowed him to see what lay before him, which was, in fact, nothing. Just more flat desert floor, rocks, scrub, stretching out into the gloom.

Exhaustion embraced him.

Clouds moved back in to smother the light.

On the horizon, he thought he might have seen two pinpoints of light—maybe headlights—but maybe he was imagining it, and anyway he couldn't tell which direction they were moving, if they were moving at all.

He told himself a story. In this story Dawn was driving toward him. She had figured out exactly where he was, and she would pick him up and get them the hell out of this place and they would just keep on driving, keep driving clear through into another life.

A great peal of agony racked Oscar's body and he was flattened onto his back. And then in an instant the pain was gone entirely.

He kept his eyes open, trying to find some stars.

"Like this?" he said out loud through chattering teeth.

Name one reason why it couldn't end like this.

★ ★ ★ ★ ★

ACKNOWLEDGMENTS

The author would like to thank the following for their guidance, friendship, patience and love, as applicable: Alexander Chee, Judith Frank, David Burr Gerrard, John Glynn, Carol Kaplan, Claire Labine, Clem Labine, Eleanor Labine, Matthew Labine, Morgen Labine, Danielle Lanzet, Rose Lenehan, Ariel Lewiton, Roger Mancusi, Rose Mancusi, Tom Mancusi, Vincent Mancusi, Rick Morgan, Jessi Olsen, Felipe Serpa, Tom Paul Smith, Analuz Vizarretea, Joy Watson, Monika Woods, Kyle Lucia Wu, and the staffs of Hanover Square Press and St. Bartholomew's Church.